BUTTERWORTH GETS HIS LIFE TOGETHER

A COMEDY NOVEL

BUTTERWORTH GETS HIS LIFE TOGETHER*

But it falls apart before he can show his friends!

BILL BUTTERWORTH

MULTNOMAH BOOKS
SISTERS, OREGON

BUTTERWORTH GETS HIS LIFE TOGETHER
published by Multnomah Books
a part of the Questar publishing family
© 1996 by Bill Butterworth
International Standard Book Number: 0-88070-987-1

Cover design by David Uttley
Cover photos by Mike Houska

Printed in the United States of America

For information:

Questar Publishers, Inc.
Post Office Box 1720
Sisters, Oregon 97759

96 97 98 99 00 01 02 03 — 10 9 8 7 6 5 4 3 2 1

BUTTERWORTH GETS HIS LIFE TOGETHER

T he whole catastrophe started out innocently enough.

I strolled down the hall of our church one Sunday after the morning service to fetch my youngest son, Bo. His class was always easy to find. Fifth-grade boys had been partitioned off from all other life forms by warning signs, flashing lights, metal detectors, and barbed wire.

This particular Sunday, however, they'd also stationed an armed guard at the entrance to the classroom. As I moved closer, I recognized Darryl Henderson, our Christian Education director, under the helmet and flak jacket.

"Morning, Bill!" Darryl declared with a grin.

"Morning to you, Darryl," I replied without one.

"Here to pick up Bo?"

Darryl paused in order to give added weight to his next words. They must teach this technique in seminary, under the heading "The Pregnant Pause."

"I guess Bo told you about George...his teacher...sad news."

Darryl knew Bo had not told me about George. But I do dumb better than most. "What's up with George?"

Darryl shook his head somberly. "It's his last week teaching fifth-grade boys. His migraines have been acting up. He's stepping down from his teaching responsibility…a great and profound loss."

I looked at Darryl blankly. Migraines and fifth-grade boys? Who'd have thunk it? But in the next split second I understood the real severity of the situation. Darryl needed a replacement—and he wanted me. We're talking about *twelve fifth-grade boys* in one pea-green room for fifty-five minutes with no chips or TV—the Protestant equivalent to purgatory.

Darryl spoke up again, just as the sound of a brawl broke out in the room behind him. "Uhh, Bill, I was wondering…the staff wanted me to ask you…uhh…if you would consider teaching this class. You're perfect for this type of ministry." He shuffled his body to block my vision from the door. "The boys would just love you and look up to you and you'd be their model, their hero. Soooo, whaddya think?"

I knew exactly what I thought. Teaching fifth-grade boys was a job that demanded superhuman physical strength, uncanny mental capabilities, the ability to tolerate paper wads packed with gum—all linked with an intense love for both Christ and pain. But not necessarily in that order.

I wasn't the guy for the job.

But how to tell Darryl? I opted for the man-of-few-words approach. "No, Darryl."

"No what, Bill?"

"No, *thank you,* Darryl," I replied.

"Are you saying you won't teach your own son's class?"

"I'd love to," I lied. "But my weight-loss coach at the gym warned me about spending time with groups of youth in social settings. You see, it revives all my bad memories from being a fatso as a kid, and then I get bad dreams, and then I go to the cupboard and I start to—"

"Well, I must admit, I'm very disappointed, Bill. I'm sure we can work some—"

"Sorry," I said, looking past him to the classroom door. "Bo! Let's hurry, buddy!" The best plan now was *speed.* Get in, get out, one quick sortie.

But Bo is a typical ten-year-old—not always the quickest to drop everything and run when Daddy beckons. And this moment was a particularly inopportune time for Bo to pretend he didn't hear me. Then I realized he probably *couldn't* hear me, since a long-haired kid with earrings in both ears had him in a headlock.

Just as I feared, this gave Darryl a chance to reload.

"Well, Bill, I don't need to give you any lectures on commitment to Christ and his church. But I do want to ask you one other question. I'm assuming you're making plans to attend our Men's Retreat next weekend, but I didn't notice your name on the sign-ups."

Now *I* had a pregnant pause. I had no intention of going to the Men's Retreat, but suddenly I felt trapped. Wouldn't it be a total breech of spiritual etiquette for me to turn down two church requests in a row?

"Oh yeah, I'm going to the retreat!" I blurted. "In fact, after I pick up Bo, I was headed over to the registration table to sign up. I wouldn't miss it."

Darryl gave me a smile, that pastoral smile that once again puts a fellow in favor with God and church staff.

I dodged the fifth-grade bullet, but clearly I'd been wounded by the retreat shrapnel. The thought of spending a weekend in close quarters with a bunch of men appealed to me about as much as a weekend in war-torn Bosnia.

Now, a weekend retreat with a bunch of women had great promise. Don't get me wrong. It's just that being a single dad, with my one daughter Betsy away at college and four sons living at home, my whole life already *is* a men's retreat.

I was still trying hard to forgive Darryl the next Friday afternoon as I drove my four boys, BJ, Brandon, Ben, and Bo, to friends' houses for the weekend.

At least the conference grounds were only a thirty-minute drive from our small town of Pine Woods in Central California. Camp Am-Zing-Grass, named for the hymn "Amazing Grace," had its syllables divided up by a turn-of-the-century Christian camp director who wanted to give it a feel that would be clever (failing to realize it might be offensive to our Native American brothers and sisters).

Once my boys were all safely handed off, I reluctantly loaded my trusty 1989 maroon four-door Honda Accord with an array of mismatched bags. I had arranged to carpool with two of my buddies. Edmund Holmes was waiting next door for me to pick him up. His mother and father had been my neighbors for many years. After we loaded his bags in the trunk, Edmund jumped in on the passenger side.

Tom Graham lives down the road just a few blocks from me. Tom has always been my hero. Well, sorta. At forty-eight, he looks ten years younger than I do at a paunchy forty-three. Tom has it all, and no paunch. He loves God, plus he used to play for the Dodgers—and the way I see it, that's all there is to a great life.

When we arrived, Tom was already standing at his curb, his matching bags adorned with the Dodgers logo. Tall, tan, strong, handsome—if Tom wasn't sort of nice, a lesser guy like me could hate him. But I mostly admired him. In fact, I mostly wished I could be just like him.

Tom got in the back of the Honda, and the three of us were off. "This should be fun!" he gushed. Edmund and I exchanged grimaces and rolled our eyes.

Tom acted as navigator. "Take Highway 49 north to Route 20," he called from behind a map. "Then stay on that road until you see the Snowshoe Cutoff."

If we're lucky, we'll get lost, I thought.

"So how's every little thing going, Bill?" Tom asked.

I squirmed a bit in the driver's seat. Why not just tell him the truth: I can't get *any* little thing together.

In fact, just yesterday I'd received an invitation in the mail for my twenty-fifth high-school reunion. I grew up back east but moved to the West Coast so I wouldn't run into anyone from the William Tennant High School class of 1970. What would my classmates think if they could see me now? What would Tom think if he knew the truth?

I should just tell it to him straight: I'm out of shape and underpaid, clueless about raising kids, and I live in constant fear of getting fired. I'm never going to get to number two of the thirty-seven entries on my list of needed house repairs that I don't know how to do...

"Never been better, Tom," I said with flourish.

"I'm really looking forward to this weekend, too," he bubbled from his spot in the back. "I've heard really good things about the speaker. A great topic *and* a really great guy!"

"What *is* he speaking on?" Edmund asked.

I shrugged my shoulders. "Don't ask me."

"Oh man, it's a great theme." Tom interjected. "The topic is *Get It Together!*"

Suddenly I had a knee-jerk reaction that caused me to speed up just as we came to the Snowshoe Cutoff. The three of us watched as the road to camp whizzed past the left side of the car.

"I'll turn around," I volunteered sheepishly. What I really wanted to say was, "Let's keep going straight and we'll be in Nevada in an hour. We can go to one of those hotels in Reno and have steak and eggs for ninety-nine cents."

A whole weekend on how to get it together. . .yikes! This had the makings of seventy-two hours of intensive guilt.

Did I need to get it together? Yes.

Did I want to? It all depended. Would it hurt?

Soon we were heading down Snowshoe Cutoff. I swallowed hard when I saw the sign that said, *Camp Am-Zing-Grass—100 yards on the right.* I sensed Edmund's muscles tightening as well.

"Howdy and welcome, y'all," bellowed a fellow dressed in jeans, red flannel, and red cowboy boots. "I'm Dusty and I'll be your trusty guide for the weekend. Once you guys are all signed up inside there, they'll point y'all to your very own digs. Yer in for one hollerin' good weekend!"

I wished I shared even half of Dusty's confidence.

How would I begin to have a hollerin' good time, I mused, while sitting around with fifty other sweaty guys who've now dropped their personal hygiene another notch? Why can't I glorify God sitting in the most worshipful of positions—sprawled in my lovely, imitation-leather recliner in my family room? Why can't the Naugahyde upholstery that envelopes my body be my sackcloth and ashes, as I sit humbly in front of the TV?

Some of my greatest achievements took place in that chair. I witnessed the moon landing, caught five minutes of the Watergate hearings, slept while Reagan debated Carter, tuned in to Desert Storm once, and memorized *Forrest Gump* on video...all from the comfort of that cracked plastic seat. If only those two bun-shaped indentations in that chair could talk, the stories they would tell.

But now, it was time to officially sign up for the "You're a Sorry Excuse for a Man" retreat. And it was becoming clear that God, in his sovereignty, allowed us to bring Tom in our car—otherwise Edmund and I would be slopping up the last of our eggs with a roll, maybe contemplating ordering another cheap Reno steak.

As I shuffled in the doorway of the registration cabin, I identified the registrar as none other than Darryl the Guilt-Meister himself. He smiled broadly as I dragged myself up to the front desk. This is why guys like him go to seminary—to learn how to get slow-witted guys like me to give up a weekend with my recliner and remote.

"Well, greetings, Bill, Edmund, Tom! It's truly fantastic to see you three here! Just need to check my paperwork, then I'll give you your cabin assignments." "Checking of paperwork" was code for finding out who still owed money and I knew, once again, I was dead in the water.

"It appears that Edmund and Tom are all paid up. But Bill, you seem to owe a little money yet."

"How much?"

"Actually, you owe the entire amount—two hundred dollars, plus a fifty-dollar late registration fee. Will you be paying by cash or check?"

I couldn't answer right away. I'd gone into financial shock, and as a result, into denial. All I could think of was the sinfully irresistible urge to eat a Tastykake. (Growing up in southeastern Pennsylvania gave me a great love for these cakes, native to Philly and simply exceptional. I had a box of the them hidden in the trunk.)

"I left my checkbook out in the car," I finally muttered. "I'll be right back." Turning on my heels, I marched out to the Honda. I popped the trunk, found my Tastykakes, and quickly downed three. Feeling just a little guilty, I grabbed my checkbook and silently prayed, *Dear Lord, just get me through this weekend and I promise to get my life together.*

Of course I have prayed a prayer like that about two thousand times in my life. I have promised God everything from foreign missionary service in Indonesia to a celery diet to a life of celibacy.

When I reentered the registration cabin, Darryl was making the cabin assignments. "Edmund, you and Bill will be in the 'David cabin'— we call it 'the cabin after God's own heart.' You go down Old Testament Road here, past the Pentateuch section of cabins. You'll want to look for the three simpler cabins on the left side of the road. You're in between 'Saul' and 'Solomon.' Remember, guys, if you start seeing the names of prophets—major or minor—you've gone too far."

"I'm in 'Moses Manor,'" Tom chimed in, suddenly realizing he was in nicer digs, "so you can take me that far down the road, I'll unload my gear, and then you guys can find your place."

I picked up a program for the weekend but didn't have the heart to look at it there on the spot. The words *Get It Together* glared up at me. We got back in the car, drove down Old Testament Road, and found

Moses Manor. As Tom got out, I couldn't help but notice how run-down his cabin appeared. Edmund must have had the same notion. "These are the *deluxe* cabins? Whoa, Nellie!"

Edmund loves expressions like "Whoa, Nellie."

A little further down the road we came to the Three Kings Cabins. Sure enough, right in the middle stood "David." It was *not* a cabin after God's own heart.

As every realtor knows, "rustic" is a semantical trick for "dump." Naked light bulbs, plumbing from Prohibition, tables and chairs from the Donner party. And then there were the beds—the oldest objects in the cabin. A pungent odor of mold, mildew, mothballs, mice—and men on retreat—pervaded the air.

Edmund and I dumped our stuff in the center of the room. The air in the cabin, if you could call it *air,* was freezing. So we looked for the thermostat. We found it on the north wall, and I turned it on high. The strong smell of propane told us we would soon be warm…and dead.

By now it was approaching quarter of six. Dinner was in fifteen minutes. Edmund picked the bed with the blue chenille bedspread that he said reminded him of one he had growing up as a kid. That left me the bed covered in a faded, rose-colored quilt with Amish designs. It wasn't the spread that bothered me as much as the large canyon down its center.

Edmund and I hustled over to the dining hall, where a large wooden banner hung from the front door read, "The Loaves and Fishes." Inside, rows of long, plain, wooden tables, with accompanying long, plain, wooden benches reminded me of a dining hall you'd see in the movies…*prison movies.* Large bowls of steaming food already sat on the tables.

But steam can lie.

I took my seat in hopes of every guy's favorite meal—barbecued pork ribs. This item is one of the last bastions of sexist eating. Few women get excited by the thought of a plate full of greasy, slimy, charcoaled ribs of pork, with sauce dripping off elbows. Men, however, know that this is where beer companies stole the phrase "It don't get no better than this."

We got seated and bowed our heads as our pastor prayed a blessing on the weekend, the men, and the food. As we all said "Amen," the bowls of steam were finally identified. *Vegetables.*

I'll eat vegetables only in order to be an example to my children. But my children were nowhere in sight. If I was going to have to get it all together, first I wanted to eat something bad for me. I hinged my hopes on the main dish. No luck! Baked, skinless chicken breasts. We were doing the unthinkable—eating healthy at a men's retreat!

Dessert was frozen fruit bars. I was about to ask Tom if he knew of any sort of refund policy for the retreat, but he had his mouth full of broccoli.

Was I the only guy bummed out by the health-clinic menu? Either I *was* the only one—or I was on retreat with a lot of nineties men who managed to miss the nineties and never learned to express as well as any female how they *really* feel about things.

Then it hit me clear as day. I was surrounded by men who tried to weasel out of teaching Sunday school!

Maybe it wasn't too late to tell Darryl I changed my mind.

2

We moved from the dining hall to the meeting room in almost perfect single file. Out of fifty-plus guys, only four walked side by side to the meeting. Men are loners. We walk by ourselves. Talking is unnecessary, a distraction. I mean, do you want to talk or do you want to walk to the meeting?

I followed Edmund down the path, face forward, head tilted down. All I could see were the whites of his Nikes and the blue of his jeans. Why do guys our age still wear jeans? I could barely breathe when the top snap was fastened, yet I insisted that they were the most comfortable pants made.

Soon we arrived at the meeting room. Edmund paused before entering and looked at me with an it's-too-late-to-turn-back-now expression on his face. We both took long, deep breaths, as if there were no oxygen in Christian camp meeting rooms. Our lungs full, we walked through the threshold of the room to the sounds of guitars being tuned, chairs being rearranged, and mikes being tested.

I always find this premeeting preparation amusing. No matter how much he tunes in advance, the guitar player will have to retune his guitar four to five times during the singing. And the mikes! Why does the protocol of any meeting involving a sound system include at least one ear-splitting shriek? Maybe the man at the soundboard falls on the knobs, sliding them all up to maximum decibel levels. I've reached the only possible conclusion that allows sound people to maintain their dignity. It has to be a nap, right?

Edmund and I shuffled in and quickly assessed that if we acted with speed, we could still procure the best seats in the room. We greeted no one, fearing distraction. We fixed our eyes on the back row where two folding chairs circa 1903 begged the question, "If you sit on me, can I hold your weight?"

We took the risk.

I turned my attention to the front of the room. At the center of the platform stood our worship leader, Bartholomew. Quite tall and thin, Bartholomew looked like one of his guitar strings taught to stand up.

Bartholomew Longhitano was the child of Italian immigrants who moved from Italy to New York before Bartholomew was born. He grew up in the Bronx, moving to California after graduation from college. (By the way, if you haven't noticed yet, *no one* over twenty-one who lives in California was born here. There must have been birthing quotas back during the baby boom. This would be before Ronald Reagan was governor, of course.)

Anyway, back to the world's tallest and thinnest guitar player. He took great pride in his heritage, as well as his name, even though it must have been brutal filling out forms in triplicate. Therefore it was a sin to call Bartholomew "Bart." He would tell you so, if you dared to get casual with this guy.

As we watched him, he was meticulously going over the order of songs with Gordon, a balding, wide fellow who would be in charge of the overhead projector and transparencies. This, too, proved an exercise in futility, since during the first number we sang, as if on cue, Gordon dropped all the other transparencies on the floor. Naturally, the rest of the songs would be out of order.

We attempted to fake it when we sang "Lord, I Lift Your Name on High," but when it came to an old hymn, most of our group was lost. Only the seven guys in the room over sixty knew "Crown Him With Many Crowns." The rest of us stared at the words to "I Have Decided To Follow Jesus."

Soon the agony of men who cannot sing, but who were singing, ended. As the screen was lowered, a giant banner became noticeable for the first time along the front wall of the pine-paneled room. Emblazoned on the red banner were large block letters painted in bold black. JESUS SAYS, "GET IT TOGETHER!"

I swallowed hard and said to myself, "I must be brave."

I looked down at my program as many other guys had done. The front page said:

GET IT TOGETHER
A WEEKEND RETREAT WITH KENNY KRAMER

Edmund nudged me with his red, San Francisco 49er-sweatshirted elbow, pointed to the name "Kenny Kramer" on the program, and silently mouthed to me, "Who's he?" Turning the page, our question was answered by Kenny Kramer's press release:

OUR SPEAKER

Kenny Kramer is taking America by storm with his speeches, books, and tapes on the topic of Get It Together! A graduate of the University of Washington, Talbot Theological Seminary, and the University of Aberdeen (Scotland), Dr. Kramer, or just plain "Kenny," as he is known to his friends, is eminently qualified to speak to the issues troubling Americans today.

He has appeared on the numerous television shows including *The Oprah Winfrey Show*, *The 700 Club*, *The Danny Bonaduce*

Show, The Tony Campolo Variety Show, and *Good Morning, Good Christians.*

His radio credits include *Larry King Live, Chapel of the Air, Rush Limbaugh, Howard Stern,* and *Focus on the Family* with Dr. James Dobson.

Kenny has authored dozens of books, articles, and his real literary love—pamphlets. His latest book, *Get It Together, America!,* has been published in over three dozen languages and is an international best-seller.

Kenny is happily married to Katie and they have six children, five girls and one boy: Karis, Kaylynn, Kelsey, Kylie, Kristyl, and Kenny VII. They make their home in Lake Oswego, Oregon, where the Kramers breed ducks, play racquetball, and raise barns.

You, too, can have Kenny participate in your next major meeting. Call our toll-free number (800-555-KENY) for more information on a Kenny Kramer event in your hometown. We'll send you brochures, letters of endorsement from people you respect, and a handsome, thirty-page, full-color handbook explaining our personalized fee structures. Don't delay, do it right now!

Kenny has met four living U.S. Presidents and Frank Peretti!

I slowly turned to the back of the room and saw exactly what I expected to see—an entire table covered, yea, *overflowing* with Kenny Kramer propaganda. I saw Kenny's face plastered all over tapes, books, videos, magazines, and comic books. Alongside them sat Kenny Kramer T-shirts, sweatshirts, mugs, Frisbees, plaques, and even tiny Kenny Kramer action figures.

So which guy in the room is Kenny? I wondered. The answer was easy, of course. Kenny would be the only gent in the joint who came dressed up. Sure enough, up on the front row, I saw a man in a heavily starched Ralph Lauren polo dress shirt in subdued pink. His khaki trousers were impeccably creased and cuffed. His loafers were complete with the little kiltie-tassel-things and from the rear I saw that his hair was hair-sprayed into a wonderful wave. You could surf off this guy's head.

I'd thought I smelled cologne when I came in, and now I believed I'd discovered the most likely source. I craned my neck to see that Kenny was holding on his lap a Bible that looked like an Atlanta phone book, except in a handsome, burgundy leather binding.

Kenny rose from his chair to a thundering ovation. Once he turned around, I saw a guy who looked just like his picture on the thousand items in the back——masculine, handsome, fit, and trim. He had too-blue eyes and his toothy smile told me he probably bought caps with the royalties from the Swahili translation of *Get It Together, America!*

I sighed. Kenny Kramer wouldn't be embarrassed to go back to his high-school reunion. Suddenly I felt hungry, tired, and nervous about this weekend. I decided to pray a silent prayer: "Dear Lord, you know I need a little help with my attitude here. If I'm honest, I probably need to hear what this guy has to say. I don't need it as much as Edmund. But I guess I do need it a little bit. I love you, Lord. Thank you. Amen."

I turned my attention to Kenny. By now he was well into his presentation, sweat appearing on his brow, and dark-pink circles appearing under his arms. The more he talked, the larger those dark circles grew. I predicted he'd soak his entire shirt before he was out of point number two.

"Is your life missing something?" Kenny pressed. "Are you disorganized, lacking in productivity, and frantically frustrated?"

As my eyes panned around the room, no one seemed immune from Kenny's barrage. Heads dropped in record numbers, at startling speeds, and men stared at their laps as if the answer to life might be found on their upper thighs. A few guys did more of a looking-around-the-room thing. To my amazement, some men actually wiped tears from their eyes.

If a guy cries in front of a woman, he can attempt the something-flew-into-my-eye explanation, but in a room full of guys, we *all* know what's going on. It's tears, man, tears.

I remember crying when my mother died. But I also remember looking around to see if anyone else noticed I was crying. Even in the midst of intense grief, I was still looking for the opportunity to produce one more major bluff. ("I'm not crying, it's allergy season, you silly person!")

I've perfected the many lines necessary to convince someone I'm not crying. I find the movie theater is an excellent practice field for these sorts of maneuvers. For example, I had a horsefly enter my eye when Robin Williams had to leave his kids in *Mrs. Doubtfire*. That insect produced a stream of protective tears that I feel is responsible for eventually saving my eyesight.

Still, Kenny kept pushing. "Men, are you feeling fulfilled in your life?

"Physically?

"Mentally?

"Spiritually?"

The use of these last three words with effective pauses between them had every guy taking stock of his own life. Unfortunately, this topic was painfully close to home. We all felt a serious need to get it together.

In a rare act of bravery, I lifted my head to look straight at Kenny. To my amazement, I saw a man who appeared to be incredibly sincere. This did not seem to be a rehearsed, canned performance. He looked like he might genuinely care about each of us. He didn't want us to live messed-up lives anymore. Even more significantly, he was telling us that the Lord didn't want us to live like that anymore, either.

Kenny asked us to bow our heads for a closing prayer. "I want you to ask God to help you get it together this weekend. Only you know if you need help physically, mentally, spiritually, or a combination of the three. If you want God's help in getting it together this weekend, I want you to lift up your hand right now, right where you sit."

He intended for all of us to keep our heads bowed and eyes closed. But as I lifted up my hand, I spontaneously opened my eyes to look around. And, sure enough, just about every guy had his hand up...and his eyes open.

As the session concluded, I looked over at Edmund, who was equally pensive. "This guy's got us right where he wants us," I mumbled to my right. "He's got a room full of messed-up guys, and we'll do whatever he asks us to the rest of the weekend."

3

As Edmund and I started the hike back to the David cabin, our bodies were drop-dead weary, but our minds pumped with excess mental energy. We were both processing Kenny Kramer's call to "Get it together." On a scale of one to ten, with ten representing the most together, I rated my best friend to be about approximately a two, and I would have to honestly place myself in the area of negative three.

I had trouble getting it together even when I was a kid. But do you know any kid who sailed smoothly through his childhood who was not heavily medicated?

Kids have the eye of an eagle when it comes to physical imperfection. And then they possess the vocal chords of a hyena as they heckle us imperfect ones throughout our growing up years.

—Your ears are too big!
—You have buck teeth!
—You're pigeon-toed!
—You have a lisp!
—You have acne!
—You have knock-knees!

—You have a mole!

—You have to wear thick glasses!

—You wear braces...on your legs!

And, of course, the words I have carried with me through the years..."You're FAT!"

I was the little fat kid that nobody wanted to choose for our sand-lot game at the ballfield next to the convent. The kids always told me to play ball with the nuns. I tried to explain that nuns don't play baseball, they play field hockey...

I do remember being fairly intelligent in school, but since boys weren't supposed to be smart back then, this created tension as well. If a geek like me knew the answer to a teacher's question, and he raised his hand to expound on his innate knowledge, he'd be turned into corn-meal over recess.

It doesn't take long for a child of any intelligence to conclude that truly smart boys are silent boys.

However, a boy *was* expected to excel in physical education class. But when you weigh the same as the rest of the boys in the class—com-bined—it makes for a little stress.

"Touch your toes, Butterworth!" Mr. McCormick, my phys-ed instructor would bark. I'd bend over as far as I could, but he'd keep shouting at me that he'd asked for toe-touches, not knee-touches.

Interesting ducks, those phys-ed teachers. In 1965, Mr. McCormick was a perfect specimen of a man. He stood about six-feet, three inches, dark brown hair in a modified crew-cut coiffure, always wearing the same outfit—a white cotton golf shirt that fit tightly enough to display the washboard abs. Khaki pants completed the uniform, with white socks and black high-top Converse All-Stars.

Ah, Converse...Do you remember those shoes? These go back way before Nike, Reebok, or even Adidas. It was a big day—a veritable rite of passage—when a boy traded in his U.S. Keds for a pair of Converse All-Stars. It was like living alone in the jungle for three days and nights, returning to the village a man.

I looked over at Edmund and recalled a recent heated discussion over the high-top, low-top controversy of 1965. Edmund, a loyal low-top man, explained to me that this was simply the shoe style of choice where he went to school. I laughed in derision and told him what we did to boys who didn't wear high-tops. The punishment involved boxer shorts, the showers, a hair net, and the girl's locker room.

Edmund and I have had some intense arguments about other child-hood issues as well. Our most severe was, "Who had it worse—a really fat kid or a really skinny kid?" Edmund was known as "The Zipper" as a boy.

We entered our cabin, pulled the string that turned on our naked overhead light bulb, and started getting ready for bed. We hadn't really talked since the end of the meeting, so I decided to break the silence.

"What are you thinking about, Edmund?"

"Just some of the stuff the speaker talked about tonight."

"Yeah, me too."

"He gave us a lot to deal with, you know?"

"I know, buddy." I paused and took a deep breath. "The truth is, there was probably no one in that room who wants to get it together more than I do."

Edmund turned and looked me in the eye for the first time. (Guys don't look at one another when they talk. This makes it *really* effective when we do…you know, high drama.)

"Really, Bill? What's up?" he asked.

"Edmund, I *do* want to get it together. I've wanted that all my life. On the way up here, I kept looking through my rearview mirror at Tom Graham sitting in the backseat of my car. I just kept thinking, *He's got it all together.* Wouldn't you agree?"

Edmund's silent nod was enough reassurance to keep my midnight confession going. "That's the kind of life I want. I want people to look at me and say, 'There's Bill Butterworth. He's got it together.' But I have a feeling that now people look at me and say, 'There's Bill Butterworth—poster boy for a messed-up life.'"

"I think you're being a little hard on yourself, Bill."

"Maybe, but that's how I feel. Plus, my high-school reunion is coming up back in Philly next month, and they want *me* to make a few remarks! I was dumb enough to tell them I was a *speech* teacher. I was a mess back in high school and if I go back there in the shape I'm in, they'll all be convinced that nothing's changed."

"Whoa, Nellie, Bill!" Ed exclaimed. "How'd you get yourself into that? You'll do fine. Hey, buddy, I feel like a failure sometimes, too. My wife was kinda getting on me the other night for some things I've been promising to do but never got around to."

"Jenny was getting on you?" I repeated in disbelief. Jenny was the sweetest woman I had ever met, and I knew from years of friendship with Edmund that the two of them rarely had words with each other.

"Yeah, she had every right to say something. I've told her for years I was going to start working out. A colleague of hers down at the junior high had a heart attack last year, and it scared Jenny out of her gourd. She's says a CPA like me is a prime candidate for a heart attack. She pictures me sitting around motionless at a desk all day."

"*Do* you move around a lot?" I asked.

"No, I basically sit at my desk all day."

"So she's right, then."

"She's always right, Bill. You were married long enough to know that. Anyway, it all erupted last year when I came back all excited from that Promise Keepers rally."

"You were pumped up," I recalled.

"Right. So, anyway, I come home from that weekend, take Jenny out to dinner and tell her I'm a new man. I tell her I was in a stadium full of guys who really love God, and we're all gonna be better men, and better Christians, and better fathers, and better husbands because we're gonna start keeping our promises."

"So what happened?" I pushed further.

"She says she's real happy for me and it's exciting to know that I'm going to keep my promises, because I have promised her for years that I would start working out so I don't have a heart attack. She says she couldn't be happier. She's hugging and kissing all over me, right there in the middle of the restaurant, really happy."

Edmund paused a second, then continued.

"So I get home from dinner that night, and I dig up the notebook that has the seven promises of a Promise Keeper. And as I read them, I notice that none of them really cover working out. So that night in bed, before we turn out the light, I decide to pass on that little technicality. Jenny flips out. She starts referring to me as the 'dead Promise Keeper' since I'm gonna kill myself by not taking care of my health…

"I'll tell you, Bill, it was a rough night, and not just because I slept on the couch."

Silence reigned in the David cabin. We both realized that we had shared more intimately in the last fifteen minutes than we had in the last six months. Here we were spilling our guts like two guys in a foxhole. Man, that Kenny Kramer was effective!

The next morning promised a chamber of commerce Sierra Nevada day. The sun was sparkling off the freshly fallen snow, icicles gleaming off the Old Testament cabins like a picture postcard. Even "rustic" can look good with a blanket of white powder.

We dressed quickly, thanks to our oversleeping, no hot water, and a man's need for a morning pot of coffee to course through his veins.

Coffee. It's the one thing a Christian can get away with in excess that doesn't get him in trouble with the elders of his church. First, many elders put away a pot or two themselves, and second, they've read the modern account of Matthew's gospel: "Do not judge lest you be judged yourselves. Why do you look at the coffee cup in your brother's hand, but do not notice the coffee pot that is in your own?"

Edmund was as committed to the nectar of the black bean as I was. He threw on a red plaid flannel shirt, while I wore exactly what I wore the night before. After all, this was a men's retreat, right?

We hustled over to the dining hall to see the graven image—a coffee urn large enough to serve the children of Israel during the Exodus, with enough left over for most of Pharaoh's army. It was a huge silver barrel with the black plastic spigot that poured the rivers of living caffeine.

The next issue was what to pour the coffee in. Edmund and I had brought our own mugs the size of thermoses. Our experience told us that most places have cups that are socially acceptable, but nowhere near large enough.

An older, volunteer staff member of the camp stood right next to the urn as I poured myself a "cup."

"Is this Starbucks Coffee?" I asked, believing the verse that says "You have not because you ask not."

The man shook his head and clucked his tongue in an unmistakable mark of disgust. "Absolutely not," he replied with the zeal of an evangelist. "Starbucks is New Age."

I looked up at him to see if he was kidding. He wasn't.

I started getting hot under the Cowboy-sweatshirt collar. I wanted to tell him that it was all right to picket abortion clinics, boycott Satanic soap companies, vote out all the liberals who want to drown us in taxes that pay for self-esteem studies, and avoid sexually suggestive shock-jock radio shows, but, for heaven's sake, DON'T MESS WITH MY COFFEE, MAN!

This is what I wanted to tell him, but I quickly realized I might be kicked out of camp for adhering to such radically heretical views, and the freshly fallen snow would mean I'd spend half the day trying to put chains on the tires of my Accord. So, I bit my lip and politely asked, "So what brand of coffee are you serving?"

The old man's face changed from wrinkled scowl to joyous smile in a split second. "Sonny, this here is 'Gospel Bob's Coffee.'"

I took one sip to see if Starbucks should be looking over their shoulders. They were safe.

"Tell me about 'Gospel Bob,'" I asked the old timer.

"Gospel Bob used to come to this camp for years as a speaker," my new friend began. "He was a dynamic speaker, just like this fella that's with your group this weekend. One year he took a short-term missionary trip to Colombia down in South America. He ran into some businessmen down there who were looking to break into the North American market with their brand of coffee. Bob and them got together and the rest is history."

The man smiled and winked knowingly, now that I was in on the brief history of Gospel Bob.

"What are we drinking this morning?" I inquired.

"This is a new flavor we're trying. Bob calls it the *Corinthian Kick*, which is part of a new line of stronger coffees that he's pitching in the exclusively Christian market."

By now Edmund had found a spot at one of the long tables, and I walked over to join him. He was eating a banana and a bran muffin, nursing his own thermos of Gospel Bob's java. One look at his banana and my mind wandered back to my house. *I wonder how the boys are doing?*

We live in a house that has an apparent ban on ripe bananas. Don't get me wrong, I buy bananas at the grocery store all the time. Brandon loves sliced banana on his Special K, which he eats at the rate of approximately one box per meal. The problem with bananas is that we can't ever seem to meet together at that precise moment when the banana is ripe. We always miss it, by being either early or late. In other words, we don't see yellow bananas at our house. Our bananas are one of two colors: green or brown.

No sooner did I get settled on the uncomfortable bench when a loud bell began to ring, signaling the first session with Kenny Kramer was about to begin in the meeting room. (Why is it that wherever you are, you're being beckoned to a place somewhere different? You don't even need a bell. You're at home, and all you can think about is the work that needs to be done at the office. You're at work, and all you can think about is what you need to do when you get home. You're in bed, and you think about working out. You're working out, and you yearn to be in bed.)

Edmund and I made a quick stop by the urn to refill our IV bottles, insuring enough coffee to get us through till coffee break. We hustled in hope that we could snag some back row seats again. Fortunately, God was smiling down on us, and the same two seats awaited our arrival.

I glanced at the program. This morning's session was entitled *Getting It Together Physically.* Some of the guys were excited because they thought this was a talk on sex. Most of us knew better. Kenny would most likely grill us on our spare-tire stomachs that generously hung over our collective belt buckles, our low-capacity lungs that had been producing a lot of wheezing already this weekend at the high altitude of Camp Am-Zing-Grass. And maybe he'd reveal why a man's diet causes him to smell the way he does.

Before Kenny got up to speak, Bartholomew announced that he was sending around a clipboard for men to sign up for the church men's softball team that would begin practice in the spring. "We're always looking for a few good men," Bartholomew reminded us. I shook my head. Softball for a guy in my shape is like a grandma making a date with Jack Kervorkian.

But I noticed, to my amazement, that as the clipboard made its way around the room, just about everyone was signing up. By the time the clipboard arrived in my row, it all became clear. Written at the top of the clipboarded page were the words: *If Kenny Kramer weren't a professional retreat speaker, what kind of job do you think he'd have?*

Everyone was having a little fun at Kenny's expense. By the time the list got to me, it was overflowing with suggestions:

JOBS FOR KENNY KRAMER

1. Used car salesman
2. Spokesperson for Tommy Hilfiger fashions
3. Demonstrator for any infomercial on TV
4. A coroner
5. Spokesperson for Daytimers
6. Boat captain on Disneyland's Jungle Cruise
7. Lobbyist for Lettuce

By the time it got to me all the good professions were taken, so I added:

8. President of Gospel Bob's Pyramid of Coffee

Meanwhile, Kenny was speaking intensely about the importance of fitness. He wove a tapestry of stories concerning friends and associates of his who had succumbed to various accidents, deformities, and terminal diseases as a direct result of irregular attendance at the health club.

Like most men, it's difficult for me to pay attention nonstop. Most guys adhere to the *Phase In, Phase Out* approach to listening. After years of practice, most of us know when to listen for key words and phrases that we will repeat after the message to demonstrate to those around us that we were paying attention. We know exactly when we can take a mental trip across this great land of ours, or wander through the Sahara with the French Foreign Legion, or take one small step for man, one giant leap for mankind.

This is how men process a lot of talking. It is the job of women and librarians to hang on every word.

For the Christian man, the most wonderful invention of the age was clearly the first Sunday Sermon Printed Outline. Now a man could casually peruse the church bulletin and discover the three key points the pastor would emphasize. Imagine how impressed the woman in his life would be when later he breezily dropped a reference to the sermon's main points at Sunday brunch.

Thanks to this printed outline, now a guy could spend the entire sermon refiguring Cal Ripken's lifetime batting average or Roger Staubach's career passing percentage, or how many lines from *Field of Dreams* he can quote from memory beyond the simple "If you build it, he will come" line that everyone knows.

Kenny was just about finished by the time I finished ruminating on these thoughts. Once again, he was drenched with sweat, which was better concealed this morning by his navy blue cardigan sweater with a Ralph Lauren crest of gold.

At the message's conclusion, I did a quick inventory of what I had learned from the talk that I could share with any well-meaning but nosy guys who would want to pick my brain that afternoon. I speedily chose the two phrases that I would camp on: "Get a complete physical exam from a medical doctor" and "Join a health club and use it regularly."

Two simple notions. I would do these two things—someday. A commitment impressive enough to take me through the afternoon free time without a hitch.

4

The morning message was especially hard on Edmund. After the session, and just before lunch, he shuffled back to our cabin, plopped down on the bed (which wasn't in any condition for "plopping"), and looked quite depressed.

"What's up, buddy?" I asked him. I knew what was up, but it's part of the Guy's Code of Ethics to ask, even when you know, so as to not overstep your bounds. Another code is that a guy doesn't ask a guy, "What's wrong?" This sounds like his wife. A guy always asks, "What's up?"

"You know," Edmund replied.

"Is it Kenny's message this morning?" I attempted to make this sound like a sincere question, based on a thought that just occurred to me.

"Yeah," Edmund said quietly.

We sat in silence for a little bit. This is a big deal for a couple of guys. "I kept hearing Jenny talking, even though it was Kenny up there," Edmund finally said. I resisted the Kenny-Jenny rhyme theory, sensing this was pretty serious stuff for my friend.

"She's been saying the same stuff for years and I haven't been listening. But I did hear Kenny this morning, I mean I *heard* him, Bill.

Monday morning you and I are going to get serious about our physical fitness."

I nodded in agreement, but I was somewhat troubled by the "you and I" part of the sentence. I wasn't married to Jenny. How did I all of a sudden become a part of this "fit or fat" fiasco?

But the more Edmund talked, the more I realized I had to go along—not for him, but for me. I was in worse shape than he was.

"What do you mean when you say 'get serious' about our physical health?" I asked reluctantly. I know how Edmund can be about these sorts of issues. One day he'll be a couch potato, the next day he'll be Schwarzenegger. And he always drags me along on his adventures.

"Well, for starters, we're gonna call Dr. Graydon's office and get ourselves a couple of complete physical exams."

It was the word *complete* that threw me. My mind spun out of the cabin and into some sterile, white medical exam room where the only things present were me and a huge hand clad in a milky white latex glove. I knew where the glove intended to go...

"Then, we're going to get one of those trial memberships at a health club in town, either Pine Woods Health Club or Sierra Body Maintenance. We're gonna pump iron, baby, slapping our bodies back into our college-age weight. It's gonna be the greatest!"

Edmund is one of those guys for whom, no matter what he is involved in, it's the greatest experience a man can achieve. When he bought his Lexus, it was the finest car ever made. When he took up snow skiing, it was the most amazing sport God ever created. When he found the FM radio station that plays nothing but jazz, he likened it to passing on from this world and entering the gates of glory.

But that's the problem with guys like Edmund. You talk to them the day after they've eaten at the Main Street Bistro and you're all psyched up to make dinner reservations to get in on this "pasta to die for." But by the time you can actually get yourself over to the Main Street Bistro,

Edmund has already left that restaurant in the dust, fawning all over Paradise Grille on L Street. He's done the same with just about everything else in his life except for his family and his Lexus. But I believe it's only a matter of time for the car.

He'll probably go through a midlife crisis and end up with one of those new two-seat Roadsters that Plymouth is beginning to hawk. I can already see his chest hair blowing in the breeze as he cruises around town with his shirt unbuttoned, gold chains dangling, looking for some action.

While Edmund continued to enthuse about our taut future, my mind wandered—not an uncommon practice for me when I am attempting to not hear what is being said. And Edmund was asking for a lot there. *Isn't there an easier way? Can't I purchase "Physical Togetherness in Minutes" somewhere in town, maybe with a modest down payment and then fifty-four monthly payments at a reasonable interest rate?*

I glanced down at my watch and realized with relief that I promised to call home this morning.

"I gotta go over to the pay phone and call my boys," I announced. "I'll be back later and we'll talk about this some more."

Edmund looked hurt. But part of the reason Edmund and I are such good friends is that we both know when to hold 'em and know when to fold 'em.

Once outside the cabin, I was met with the sparkling crisp mountain air that makes this part of the country so desirable. But I didn't want to return to the cabin for a jacket. That would mean I'd have to listen to Edmund for at least another ten minutes before it felt socially acceptable to walk out again.

The pay phone, weathered from the outdoor exposure, had been personally installed by Alexander Graham Bell. I placed the phone to my ear, but the freezing temperature of the receiver made my entire body flinch. I guess this explains why I dialed my home number and my credit card number only to hear the phone being answered, "Thank you for calling Domino's Pizza. May I take your order, please?"

It was *extremely* tempting to ask how far away they delivered, but I simply admitted I had the wrong number and redialed.

"Hello." It was Brandon, my sixteen-year-old. It still caught me by surprise to hear my third child sounding like he was a forty-eight-year-old man. Voice change is a cruel reality to a parent.

"Brandon, it's Dad."

"Hey Dad. What's happenin'?" Brandon always sounded low-key, the personification of "mellow."

"I'm up here at Camp Am-Zing-Grass at the Men's Retreat. It's going well, but I called to see how you guys were doing."

Silence.

"So, how *are* you doing?"

"Fine."

"Who's there?"

"All the boys."

"Can I talk to BJ?"

"Sure."

"Brandon?"

"Huh?"

"I love you."

"Here's BJ."

I guess a dad must get used to the fact that a teenager isn't always motivated to echo the words "I love you, too" back to his father. Brandon will let it slip every now and then, but it's another one of those "guy" things that men live with. BJ would be more expressive. My oldest son was already eighteen, a man himself. He was finishing up his senior year in high school, making plans for his life after graduation. I've always found this process intriguing. When a little boy is four, he wants to be a fireman, or an astronaut, or Deion Sanders. In our school district, by the ninth grade they need a little clearer direction in order to write a twenty-page paper on the career choice they've made for a class called "Life Skills." This is where the more feasible vocations of history teacher, graphic designer, or small-business owner come to light.

But something happens that senior year that I guess a psychologist would call regression. BJ is eighteen and has returned to fireman, astronaut, or Deion Sanders. Actually, I'm kidding. I'd be thrilled if that were the case—because at least he'd have decided to be *something!* It's the indecision that produces extra ulcers in my life. BJ keeps telling me he'll make up his mind soon. But it never seems to be soon enough for the parents, does it?

"BJ, it's Dad."

"Hey Pops!" BJ sounded excited to hear me, but when he calls me "Pops" I know someone other than the family is present. He thinks by calling me "Pops" he sounds powerful and so he does it to impress his friends. I need to talk to him about that. Am I the only parent who has a list of things a mile long I need to discuss with my child that I never quite get around to?

"Who's there, BJ?"

"Just the boys. And Cindy." Cindy was his girlfriend.

"Is everything going okay around there?" I asked, part of me wanting an answer, part of me wanting to bask on in ignorance's warm glow.

"Not bad," BJ responded diplomatically. "Ben and Bo have been fighting but no one got hurt and that leg on the dining room chair can be fixed with a little superglue."

I hurried on. "Did everything go all right last night?"

"Uh-huh. Bo stayed over at Scott's, Ben stayed with Ryan, Brandon was at Mark's and I stayed here. Everything's cool, Dad."

"Are you sure?"

"Dad, you worry too much. Like I said, the only damage was a broken leg—on a chair, not a kid. I thought you'd be real proud of us."

"I am proud of you, son." I flinched. I hate it when one of my kids has to hint around for a compliment.

"Oh, you did get a phone call earlier this morning from back east," he added.

"Who was it?" I asked.

"A lady. I wrote her name down somewhere…" His voice trailed off as he went hunting for the paper with the name on it. "Ahh, here it is, Pops. Her name is Lynne Merton."

Lynne Merton. I hadn't heard that name in twenty-five years. "What did she want, BJ?"

"She wanted to know for sure if you were planning on attending the high-school reunion back in Philadelphia. And something about you speaking."

"What did you say to her?"

"I told her that I doubted it, since you were currently unemployed and living off welfare."

"BJ!"

"And I told her you were divorced, and you hadn't had a date in *years,* and since you had put on so much weight, if you came you would have to fly first class because you can't fit in those seats back in coach."

"BJ, you're not serious, are you? I can't believe you'd tell a stranger all that hooey." I was hoping for the best here.

BJ decided to keep me in suspense by changing the subject. "Cindy and I are just getting ready to go out to a matinee with the younger two. You wanna talk to them real quick?"

"Yes, thanks, BJ, you're a good man!"

"Hi Dad, it's Bo," my ten-year-old announced. Ironically, he's the only one I don't need an introduction from, since he's the only guy left in the house whose voice hasn't changed.

"Hey, buddy, how ya doing?"

"Dad, when Ben gets on the phone, would you tell him that I was playing with the Game Boy first, and he has to wait until I get killed in my game before he can just take it away?" Bo is all boy, typically ten, meaning he is hopelessly addicted to video games. It's his life, nothing else matters, with the possible exception of TV.

"Okay, buddy, I'll talk to him." I paused. Fortunately, I can still be lovey-dovey with my ten-year-old. "I love you and I miss you, Bo. But I'll be home soon...tomorrow afternoon, okay?"

"I miss you too, Dad. I'll see you tomorrow. Pay attention in the meetings, okay?"

That might sound like an unusual request from a fifth-grader, but the last time I was at a PTA meeting, I fell asleep. And, okay...so I drooled a little. A natural human function. But embarrassing words made their way to Bo's classroom. Parents can be so cruel.

I have to give Bo credit, though. It's quite amazing that an eight-year-old would have the presence of mind to produce the fictionalized account of his father's near-terminal battle with Sleeping Sickness. The Tsetse fly had made its way from Africa on a Pan Am flight, stowing away in a Nigerian's carry-on.

"Okay, Bo, I'll stay awake. Put Ben on."

"Hey, yo, whatcha know?" The voice was from my thirteen-year-old son, Benjamin. He is a bit of a kidder, but, like all my boys, has a heart of pure gold beneath the layers of sweat, grime, and officially licensed National Football League apparel.

"How are you doing, Ben?"

"Okay."

"Bo tells me that you and he are having a little disagreement over the Game Boy."

"Dad, he won't let me play with it until he's dead."

"Why is that a problem, Ben?"

"Dad, he's good at it and the game he's playing has multiple levels. He'll be playing forever."

"How many levels?"

"Thirty-six."

"Thirty-six?"

"Yup."

"Benjamin..."

"Okay, it has nine levels. But Dad, I wanna play with it."

"I understand, but we'll have to figure out another way to deal with this situation."

"I know how we can settle this," he said. "When you get home tomorrow afternoon, after you unpack and all, why don't you and me go into town and buy another Game Boy? We need some quality time together anyway, dontcha think, Dad?"

Leave it to Ben to introduce the "Dad doesn't spend enough time with us, so let's make him feel guilty and get him to buy stuff for us" shtick. Poor guy. He had no idea I was attending a retreat that made his attempts at guilt look like stickball in Shea Stadium.

"No, Ben, I don't think that's the answer. But I *will* be home tomorrow afternoon and we *will* spend some time together. You have a big social studies test on Monday, don't you?"

"Yeah," was the mumble from the phone's other end.

"Well, I'll help you study, okay?"

"Great." When called upon, Ben could generate tongue-in-cheek excitement with the best of them.

"All right. Well, I'll let you guys go on to your movie. Are you seeing something decent?"

"Relax Dad, it's PG. We won't corrupt our minds at the movie theater. We save that for school."

"Okay, Ben. I love you."

This caught Ben off guard, and he experienced mild panic. Not wanting to completely shut me down, he chose the mush-mouth response of love to a parent:

"Oshwanshannaseemako," he said, which I took to mean "I love you too, Dad." That was good enough for me.

I hung up the phone, the receiver now feeling warm and comfortable. I checked my watch. It was time for lunch. The thought filled me with an odd mix of enthusiasm and dread.

Remember when you were a little kid and your parents threw you a big birthday party? Your dad, or more likely, your mom, would sit you down before the party to give you the annual "Nice Boys Share" speech. The message was riddled with guilt-producing words and phrases, generously peppered with silent threats.

So, the one day you had every right to take the first piece of cake—and the biggest—you exercised mother-induced Christian charity by insisting that your guests be served first, with you eating the crumbs that remained. It was a backward way to spend your birthday, as far as you were concerned.

Our men's retreat revisited those feelings on that cold Saturday. We hustled over to the dining hall for lunch. (Notice I choose the verb *hustled.* This is what men do. If this were the women's retreat, I believe the active verb would be *scurried.*)

After we manned our seats at the long, narrow, splinter-ridden benches, the cooks took our breath away with a meal that met our wildest male cravings (we had griped about the food from the moment we arrived last evening). Yes, folks, it was an all-American lunch of burgers, with all the fixings, French fries, chips and dip, and ice-cream sandwiches for dessert. It was the meal of American royalty.

And when I say fixings, I'm talking melted cheese, bacon strips, and deep-fried onion rings, among other less-exciting additions like lettuce, tomato, sprouts, and carrot shavings.

The chefs, who had been hiding the entire weekend up to this point, thought this a wonderful occasion to make an entrance. Rusty, or Mr. Am-Zing-Grass, as we began to refer to him, clanged a fork against a drinking glass and asked us all to applaud the dining room staff for the fine job of food preparation this weekend. We all clapped politely.

The cooks scowled beneath their white high hats. Being a totally male staff of chefs, they understood "clapping politely." Men clap politely at the opera, for example. They clap politely when Mrs. Wiggins stands to her feet to give the annual report from the missionaries in Tunisia at the missions dinner on the second Thursday of October in the yearly calendar of church events.

The chefs look at one another in disbelief. Certainly "polite applause" was the reaction they would have expected from steamed vegetables, but there was enough cholesterol on that day's table to kill Covert Bailey.

Usually guys make noise when they applaud. We yell, we do the wave, we act like misbehaving little boys. *That* is cheering, and it's nowhere near "polite applause." But we had all been bit by The Kenny Kramer Guilt Bug.

The chefs returned to their caged kitchen in a huff. Suddenly we realized we could live to regret the weak ovation. The best meal of the weekend was being served up for us, but how could we dive into one of those artery-hardening, blood-muddying, triple-bypass-producing burgers after just hearing about how important it is to be a physical specimen that rivals a Greek god?

It was the eight-year-old birthday party all over again! One by one, our table full of men passed the tray of burgers down the line, refusing to eat one, waiting for the tray of carrots and celery, and (the ultimate hypocrisy), offering up compliments on "the yummy salad bar."

Nobody bought that line for a second. First of all, no guy ever uses the word "yummy" in a nonsarcastic sentence. Profound, life-altering questions swam around our empty heads. What if we were passing up the only decent meal of the weekend?

We searched the room, looking to and fro for one man to stand in the gap. Our collective jaws dropped when we discovered who our leader would be. To our amazement, our leader was *our leader*...

Kenny Kramer.

Over at the head table, Kenny was chowing down on a burger the size of Miami, with French fries clustering around it like the Florida Keys. Calories, cholesterol, and heart disease dripped down his fingers to his hands to his wrists to his Ralph Lauren designer cardigan.

A general hush had fallen over the room, so Kenny could be heard as he spoke to the camp director in his effervescent, bubbly form. "I haven't had a burger with all the trimmin's like this one in a long time! I'm really excited! This is quite a treat you've prepared here, Wendell! God bless you, brother!"

Once the shock of this scene was over, we guys started making eye contact with one another. What is communicated immediately between two men may take years of marriage to develop and pass between a man and a woman. To me this is one more example of the advantage of being born superficial.

The looks passed around the dining hall echoed the same sentiments:

—Kenny's one of us!

—It's okay to eat a grease-burger!

—We're all in this together!

—Eat two burgers if you feel like it!

—Kenny has to deal with this stuff, just like we do!

—It's all right to ask for extra barbecue sauce, too!

—Pig out, guys!

—Kenny's not our mother!

—Bring on the angioplasty delights!

—Even Kenny's still trying to get it together!

It was that last nonverbal message that hit me hardest. In spite of all the fun I was having at Kenny's expense, he was a regular guy. He wasn't perfect. He struggled. And even he gave in to temptation.

To the outsider, it may appear that Kenny Kramer lost his credibility, his platform, his power that afternoon in the dining hall. But that just shows why that person would be called an outsider. To us guys who know what life is all about, it shakes down differently:

We were ready to crown Kenny as our new King!

5

The title of Saturday evening's session was *Getting It Together Mentally and Emotionally*. In other words, it would have been the highlight of a women's retreat, but for a group of men, it offered all the promise of a night at the shopping mall at Christmas.

Kenny was once again in fine form, explaining to all of us how he had climbed a mountain in his free time that afternoon. He noted that it was a very typical Saturday afternoon for our speaker.

Since most of us had napped for a large portion of the free time, the only way we could relate was to remember the incredible energy it took to get out of the concave section of our mattresses. I knew I'd be feeling that physical endeavor in my stomach muscles for at least another week. One more reminder to call Dr. Graydon when I got home.

But tonight the focus were our brains and our hearts. By the time the meeting was over, we left the room feeling like the Scarecrow *and* the Tin Man rolled into one. I found this type of conversation particularly distressing, for you see, I am a purist. I look back fondly on the days when all a man had to do was lift weights, put a car engine together, and cheer on all major sports teams. The deepest we got into our brains was over discussion questions like: "Is Muhammed Ali a better fighter since he changed his name from Cassius Clay or is it all about equal?"

And in the golden days of the past, heart issues were exclusively wrapped around private events in a man's life. In rare instances, a male could express emotions like sadness, fear, and/or grief, but it was necessary to keep it brief, and the TV on.

A fair example of a "gut-wrenching" experience would be if your son was not moved up to varsity in his sport in the appropriate year. One could express heartfelt emotions of anguish in the privacy of one's home.

Kenny was recommending that we all *read books*. This caught many guys off guard, and there were even some guys who put down their *Sports Illustrated* in utter disbelief. As for me, I was comfortable with his suggestion, as I was a committed reader of the greatest writer of all time...John Grisham.

That's right. You can have your Shakespeares, your Chaucers, your Charles Stanleys, and your Max Lucados. For a guy like me there's a certain literary magic found in the two simple words *Pelican Brief*.

I'd be willing to bet you're a lot like me. I own a fairly large number of books, I just don't ever get around to reading them. I'm the victim of the latest ad campaigns that woo me to the local bookstore or newsstand. That's why I bought most of the books I did. Let's look back over the recent book-selling history:

—Ten years ago we all had to run out and buy Tom Peters' *In Search of Excellence*, but most of us were just using it as office dressing. I placed it conspicuously on the credenza behind my desk, so all could conclude I possessed one excellent business mind.

—Ditto for *One Minute Manager* and *Iacocca*. It was suicide in the workaday world if you didn't own these classics. With all three titles on your office shelf, you told the world you were committed to excellence, efficiency, and those cool-looking blue dress shirts with the white tab collars and matching French cuffs.

—How many Christian books have you bought because they were endorsed by your pastor, Billy Graham, Pat Robertson, or Promise Keepers? They look good on the shelves, don't they? Spirituality on display.

Women, on the other hand, buy books in bulk, reading seven or eight at the same time, a practice that still boggles my mind. How they can keep the commentary on Jeremiah differentiated from the biography of Corrie ten Boom, while still processing Larry Burkett's financial principles for upscale, suburban Baby Boomers, at the same time reading Janet Oke's latest prairie romance, and Martha Stewart's guide to sautéing potatoes?

Plus, they read the Bible!

When a guy buys *The One Year Bible*, he knows it's a purchase with a good ten-year life span.

Remember back in college, where the professors mercilessly demanded that entire books be read on a daily basis? It is my belief that this practice invigorates females, whereas it leaves permanent mental and emotional scars on the male of the species.

Kenny wasn't satisfied with just meddling in our lives as readers. He closed the session Saturday evening with an admonition for each and every man in the room to join a small men's group. At first I felt excluded since I am six-foot-one. But he was referring to a group of four or five men that meet weekly to pray together, talk about heart issues, and be accountable to one another on all levels.

Edmund and I glanced awkwardly at one another. We had talked about starting the same sort of group thirty-seven times in the last six months. Between conflicts with work schedules, children's routines, church commitments, naps, recliners, and another bad season for Daryl Strawberry, it just never got off the ground.

Part of the hassle was the time slot. Because of everyone's demanding schedules, the only time available was Wednesday morning at six. I couldn't believe I would ever agree to meet at that time. Back when I was a young college dude, that was about the time I went to bed! Time flies when you're deteriorating.

Later that night, as I hit the deep cavern known as the center of my mattress in the David cabin, I knew that when I got back home, it was time to start reading, stimulating my mental energies, getting into the emotional flow, and most of all, it was essential to get the small group started.

Edmund knew the same things. I know that for a fact, since we did not utter a word from the time the meeting ended till we retired that evening. For a guy, silence on subjects like these indicate agreement. You only talk when you're opposed. Our immediate mission was crystal clear—our time had come to relentlessly pursue misery.

I sighed a huge sigh as I attempted to get comfortable in "David's" bed. Thankfully, there was only one more session to go.

Sunday's sky was not as sunny as Saturday's had been. I dressed quickly, choosing the only shirt I brought that had buttons and the only pants that weren't jeans. I wondered if it *did* snow how we were going to get off the side of this mountain, and how quickly I might get a thermos of Gospel Bob's Corinthian Kick.

Bartholomew had chosen slower, hymn-type songs for us to sing that morning. This was a mistake, since most of us were pretty worn out from sleeping in the "rustic" beds. The men began to drop like flies.

By the time Kenny got up to address us for his final session, the room was in a surreal sort of glazed funk. It was clear he was gonna have to be Knute Rockne to motivate the crowd this morning.

But Kenny Kramer had saved the best for last. Looking especially dapper in blue blazer, light blue Oxford dress shirt, and gray slacks, Kenny's topic for the day was *Getting It Together Spiritually*. It was the kind of talk that grabbed us all by the nape of the neck, shook us till our pocket knives rattled, and our Bass Pro Shop Preferred Customer cards were flying around the room.

"My experience tells me this room is filled with guys who have wanted to get it together for years, but have never completed the follow-through necessary for success." Kenny scanned the room in a calculated attempt at eye contact. As if on cue, heads dropped forward in tacit agreement, like a room full of marionette puppets.

"Do you know why you can't get it together physically? Mentally? Emotionally? It's because you don't have it together *spiritually.*" The silence was incriminating. Deep down inside, we all feared he was right on target.

"Guys, trust me on this one. If you commit yourself to becoming a follower of Christ—not just a believer, but a follower—you'll have a much greater chance of things coming together for you in life. Don't misunderstand what I am saying. A Christian is never promised a problem-free life, but Christ did come to offer us abundant life while living here on earth. I'm here today to tell you that through the Lord's power you *can* get your life together!"

Edmund and I slouched down in our back-row chairs. There was nothing in Kenny's presentation that was new. We heard for the umpteenth time the value of a daily personal Quiet Time, where we could communicate with God through prayer and he could communicate to us through the Bible. We heard again about the significance of participating in our local church, and about the importance of our testimony to non-Christians.

I pondered how many times I had sat in a meeting room hearing similar words. What was it going to take to finally get my life together—and in time for my reunion?

I remember vowing to clean up my act in high school in the hopes that God would take my dateless life and turn it around to where I was having to choose between Sherry Rich and Ruth Jensen. I wanted a date with either of them more than life itself. I was only willing to be a missionary in

Africa if God could arrange for one or the other of my female loves to come along.

Had I changed?

This time it's going to be different, I admonished myself. *Butterworth, you need to get your life together, and you're going to start right now.*

I stopped slouching. I even leaned forward in my seat like an eager Baptist or a smart Dalmatian.

By the time Kenny was ready to ask guys to stand as a sign of their commitment, Edmund and I were the first two men on our feet. It was really going to work. It just had to.

Snow fell as we loaded my Honda in the bitter cold. The road conditions called for snow chains. I hate snow chains. They never fit. They're either too big or too small, and the fact that you have to put them on in sub-zero temperature is a sure way to frenzy, frustration, and frostbite.

Snow is fun when you're a kid and only when you're a kid. It's great for building snowmen, having snowball fights, and sledding. But when you're an adult, it means shoveling and snow chains. One kills your hands, the other your back.

Edmund and Tom were out there with me, and before too long we had a Moe, Larry, and Curly thing going. Three hours later, the job completed, we jumped in the car and headed for home.

Tom and Edmund fell asleep before we left the campgrounds, since they hadn't slept since Thursday night. I bravely hung in there, since it was my job to drive. I did miss the efforts of a good navigator, however, and that's the best way I can explain how I made a wrong turn early in our trek.

And that also explains how we ended up in Reno that afternoon, working our way through an all-you-can-eat buffet at a hotel. By the time we got home that night, our hearts were bursting with good intentions and our stomachs with cheap Reno steaks.

6

onday mornings are legendary for challenging one's incentive to live. The body drags, the brain is dull. Love for God is still there, but buried deeply in Monday Mud. A guy who wants to start his work week on the right foot should most likely wait an extra day.

A Monday after a regular weekend of relaxation, unwinding, and recharging is tough enough. But this Monday, after an entire weekend at Camp Am-Zing-Grass—combined with a wrong turn and the four-hour layover to pig out in Reno—started off like a prostate exam.

"Dad, I need help with my social studies homework," Benjamin whined before seven that morning. I was groggily packing four brown bags with enough prewrapped stuff to fill four boys' bellies until they could get home after school, inhale the refrigerator, and politely spit out the hardware.

"Is the homework due today?" I asked, crossing my fingers, hoping for a day or two's reprieve.

"It's due tomorrow," Ben replied, between chomps on his breakfast-on-the-run of whole-wheat toast with peanut butter and jelly, half a box of cereal, a pint of orange juice, and a granola bar. (Lord knows how much they'd eat if they ever got up early enough to actually *sit down* for a meal at the breakfast table.)

"That's good news," I sighed, grateful that I could help him with it tonight. "What kind of homework is it?"

"We're having a big test on Wednesday on the unit that covers civics and the U.S. Constitution."

"We should talk to your oldest brother BJ, since he drives a Civic," I responded with a poker face.

But Ben clearly wasn't into Honda jokes. "It's a *big* test, Dad. I need you to help me study. You've got to quiz me on the material so I can do my best."

I released a large exhale as I realized I was back home from the non-reality of a weekend retreat. Home meant having feelings like these. Without meaning to, Ben was doing what all kids do—put the pressure of a student's academic success squarely on the backs of the parents!

Why is a kid's success in school dependent on how much help he can get from Mom and Dad? Who came up with these rules? I made a mental note to stop by the library and look up *civics* in the dictionary before that evening so I had a bit of a head start on what it is that we would be studying together.

BJ and Brandon had left for high school an hour earlier. BJ's car was a 1981 silver Honda Civic wagon, affectionately known as "The Silver Bullet." Actually, the car did go from zero to sixty in a fortnight. The only truth to the name was that the car was sorta silver, if you count faded gray as part of the silver family. It was an incredible help to have one of the boys driving. With all the errands the kids can demand of you in a given twenty-four-hour period, I was down to about four hundred miles a day in local trips. BJ was responsible for the rest.

Bo, like Ben, was still young enough to ride the school bus without the fear of permanent damage to his self-esteem. Bo left for school thirty minutes after the high-schoolers, but thirty minutes before Ben.

Why can't all schools start and stop at the same time? Do we need legislation for this to occur? Is there a candidate who will step forward to make this the key plank in his or her platform? It's nutso trying to get all the kids ready for school when they operated on three different schedules! Starting all together would better prepare them for the real world of adults, be it a job or prison.

Anyway, once Ben was safely off to his bus stop with a couple of apples and a brown banana to get him through the one-block walk, it was time for me to get my act together. Like most adults I know, I must work for a living.

I used to like my job, but that was 1978. I'm one of those guys who thinks life would be infinitely better if a heavenly paycheck floated down from the sky every other week as payment for skills like eight hours of sleep and faithful service to my imitation-leather recliner.

To my way of thinking, it's clear in the Bible that Eve was the first person to eat of the forbidden fruit. It wouldn't have been Adam. Most likely, he was sitting in his recliner and did not want to expend the energy necessary to get out of his seat. Granted, he may have *asked* Eve for an apple, but even that is suspicious to me. My guess is Eve had her own sights on the apple, whereas Adam was waiting for God to create Twinkies.

The devil was smart enough to go directly after Eve with questions about the Tree of the Knowledge of Good and Evil and the Apple. If Satan had wanted to go after Adam, he would have tempted him with pro football and Fritos.

So, now that you understand the Garden of Eden better (well-worn recliners, junk food, the Green Bay Packers), let's return to the curse from the Garden—working for a living.

I have a fairly pleasant job. I am a member of the faculty at our local community college, Pine Woods College. I am part of the department of communications, where I have the distinct pleasure of teaching the courses on public speaking. I've taught for years, which means I've collected enough copies of speeches on three-by-five index cards to line them up end-to-end and go to the Senate floor and back at least thirty-nine times.

However, this in no way qualifies me to "make a few remarks." I'm speaking particularly about remarks at twenty-five-year reunions. That's the problem with a teaching job. People expect you to be able to *do* what you teach—and be good at it!

I wonder if it is too late to change professions. I'm not a quitter, but getting fired wouldn't be all that hard. The chairman of my department, Dr. Floyd, happens to be a "why hasn't he retired already?" guy who is consistently depressed—morbidly so—because he is convinced that budget cutbacks will eventually mean the complete destruction of his entire department.

Until that time, we experience gradual cutbacks each semester. Every week we attend a department meeting with Dr. Floyd that centers around who will be the next casualty, if the need for a layoff presents itself.

We all try to treat Dr. Floyd especially well. Or put another way, our department spends more time kissing up to Dr. Floyd than any other task we take on.

Another stressor is the work itself. Like most in the job force, we are vocationally challenged. That's because we are assigned more work than we can handle. That is, if you have the audacity to think you can have a life outside your job.

I go to work and face a mountain of papers to grade, reports to read, committee findings to peruse, budget proposals to analyze, and inter-office memos to trash. Then there's the classroom time. Speech is the only class where the students are given fair turnabout in torture. This means after I'd had my say, I must listen to scores of students with nothing to say, say it badly for a very long time.

So when I arrived on campus Monday morning, it was providential that the first piece of paper to receive my attention was a pink phone message:

To: Bill Butterworth

From: Edmund

Remember, today is the first day that you and I Get It Together! Show off to all your coworkers, students, and friends and make me proud.

P.S. I called and got us both appointments for complete physicals on Wednesday. Dr. Graydon can't wait to get his hands on you!

I appreciated the encouragement from Edmund, although I didn't like the way the last part sounded. Suddenly, in my mind's eye, Dr. Graydon's hands looked like catcher's mitts, ready to probe, push, and pinch where no man should boldly be allowed to go.

The second phone message was from Dr. Floyd's secretary.

To: Bill Butterworth

From: Sally, for Dr. Floyd

Just a reminder there is a full department meeting at 3 P.M. in Miller Hall, Room 339.

Be prepared to justify financial requests for next year's budget.

Meetings. Why must adults schedule these events? Is it to insure that we have physical contact with one another? With technology advancing to where it is today, isn't it intimidating enough for a boss to chew us out over the Internet?

Making matters worse, three o'clock in the afternoon was the world's worst time for a meeting. It's nap time. And Dr. Floyd's speeches were more boring than a PBS pledge drive. But, heaven forbid if you happened to doze off...

I'd always envied Joe Westman, a colleague of mine who had the uncanny ability to look intrigued with Dr. Floyd's speech while all the time napping with his eyes open. I didn't know this feat was possible. I thought sleep was like sneezing...you had to do it with your eyes closed.

The meeting was centered around the annual budget. This is the business version of a wrestler trying to make the weight limit, only to find out he's still three pounds over, so he's sent into the steam room and told to stay in there until he's lost what he needs to.

When the memo said "Be prepared to justify financial requests," that was code for "Money is tight, so unless you have the most amazing request in college history, you're not getting any."

In years past I have tried my best to fulfill the "Amazing Request" portion of the code. Nothing works. I've told Dr. Floyd stories that would reduce a criminal to tears only to have him retort, "Money doesn't grow on trees, Butterworth. You'll have to make due with what you have."

Joe Westman knocked on my office door while I was still processing the trauma of this afternoon's pending meeting. As I let him in, I realized this was my first chance at showing someone that I've got my life together since my big weekend encounter.

"Just came from Floyd's office," Joe commented in his late-night-FM disc-jockey voice. Joe makes Darth Vader sound like a soprano.

"Wait, Joe, before you go any further," I said, "I want to tell you that I just came from a weekend retreat that has been of immense help to me. I honestly believe you are going to see a different Bill Butterworth over the next few weeks. I'm working on getting my life together."

Joe stared at me with his sea-green eyes. I could tell by his look that he was trying to determine if I was serious or if this was the setup to a new joke I'd heard on the golf course. Apparently I looked believable.

"That's great, Bill. Anyway, Sally says that Floyd is coming into today's meeting with a decision to cut an additional 15 percent from the already existing budget and—"

"FIFTEEN PERCENT?!" I bellowed. "We've already reduced the budget to its bare bones. Where does he think we're going to come up with enough money to operate in any sort of efficient manner? This guy is nuts. He's too old to know what he's asking. The problem with tenure is these guys just sit around the faculty lounge waiting to die. But in the meantime they make life for guys like you and me a nightmare. How can we properly educate our students with no money? I can't believe the audacity of this guy. He's a jerk, that's all…a complete and total jerk."

Joe waited patiently for me to finish my tirade. Actually, as tirades go, this was a fine one. I paced the tiny office with the acting bravado of Charlton Heston, slammed my fist on the desk like a blond, overweight John Wayne, and threw my hands in the air in a disgusted gesture of frustration, much like Kevin Costner did when he became frustrated with the cavalry in *Dances With Wolves*.

"I can see I came at a bad time," Joe mused as he slowly began backing out of my office. "Just thought you'd want to know what's going down."

Before I had a chance to apologize, Joe was gone. As he closed the door behind him, he peeked in one last time and added, "Good luck on getting your life together."

Standing alone in the silence of my office, I realized I had blown it. I was the same old Bill, complaining, flying off the handle, stressing off the chart.

I was berating myself to myself when the phone rang.

"Bill? It's Edmund. How's it going, man?"

"Edmund, it's good to hear your voice. And I want to commend you on your perfect timing."

"How's that?"

"Not more than thirty seconds ago I had my first chance to show a colleague how I got my life together."

"Yeah?"

"Yes. And you'll be thrilled to know that he just left the office in fear for his life. I ranted and raved around the room like a maniac. It was not a pretty picture."

"That bad?"

"Let's put it this way. I looked like I would envision Tony Campolo if he ever got on hard drugs."

"Whoa, Nellie," Edmund replied earnestly, sensing the severity of the situation.

"Yeah, it's not a good way to start my new life. I turned over a new leaf and it's covered with sow bugs."

"Don't be too hard on yourself, Bill. Listen, I've got some news for you."

"What is it?" I asked.

"I've already blown it myself," Edmund admitted. "My assistant, Denise, forgot to bring me some coffee first thing, and you know how I love my morning coffee. I especially needed a cup to get started—this being Monday and us being gone all weekend till late last night."

"I understand," I empathized.

Edmund paused and then confessed, "I lost my cool. I mean, I really yelled at Denise. She ran off crying. She's still in the ladies' room trying to regain her composure."

"Tough break, Edmund," I replied, trying to sound as sympathetic as possible, but inwardly I was *thrilled* to hear that I wasn't the only dolt left on the planet.

Then Edmund added, "Well, at least I didn't march into her office and announce that I had decided to get my life together. Thank the Lord he spared me from being *that* stupid!"

Edmund's comment made me realize how God treats us all individually.

I spent the rest of the day counseling students, pow-wowing with fellow faculty members, returning calls, and answering mail. The good news was that I had no classes to teach on Mondays.

In all my rubbing shoulders with other teachers, I found no one who felt confident in getting any money out of Old Man Floyd. The geezer had effectively whipped us all into shape. The only way to get serious bucks was to move from the communications department to computer science.

By the time three o'clock rolled around, I was a little drowsy, so I tanked up on espresso, threw some NoDoze in my pocket, grabbed my notes, and headed over to the Miller Building. If I was lucky, I'd get there early enough to get a good seat. In this context, a good seat was anywhere not directly in front of Dr. Floyd.

Dr. Floyd, the quintessential picture of a college professor, shuffled through the doorway sporting his brown tweed jacket, wrinkled yellow dress shirt, khaki pants, disheveled grayish brown hair, and a pair of glasses that were so old, people still referred to them as "spectacles." He carried a manila file folder, well-worn in the exact spot in which he carried it in his hand. Within the file folder was our future, or more precisely, the lack of it. The budget proposals made a pitifully thin file for a major department in a thriving junior college.

"I have looked over all of your proposals in detail," Dr. Floyd began. Naturally, a man with so little time left on earth had no interest in small talk. "I regret to inform you that I have found no cases that merit any concentrated attention, so I am categorically denying all requests for budget increases at this time."

The room was quiet enough to hear 15 percent of the budget drop.

"Are there any questions?"

This was purely superficial on Dr. Floyd's part. He wanted to entertain questions like he wanted to bungee-jump. We all knew the drill, so we continued our posture of sleep-induced silence. You gotta love meetings for their ability to produce depression and stress all in the same agenda.

"Fine. Since there are no questions, I feel compelled to move on to the next order of business."

Joe and I looked at one another in silent communication. We knew what was coming and we were prepared for it. A moment of pity sprung up inside of me for all those who sat around the table, for they were in for an unpleasant surprise. I was simply bored by now. Dr. Floyd had a million pieces of unfinished business before he got to his announcement, and, as I feared, I began feeling very sleepy.

"Because of the financial downturn the college is currently experiencing, I have had to make a very hard decision, but I believe a sound one."

In a rare moment in department history, Dr. Floyd had everyone's attention—but mine. Later, I was told that the meeting proceeded something like this:

"I've decided that we need to make another attempt at reducing our individual budgets," Dr. Floyd announced.

The air was slowly but effectively sucked out of the room as everyone inhaled oxygen at the same time.

"How much more do we need to trim off?" a young instructor politely inquired.

Dr. Floyd was ready. "All of us need to make one more set of cuts in our budget...and I'd like you to reduce your figures by 20 percent."

"TWENTY PERCENT?!" Joe blurted out in surprise. The impact of his scream abruptly woke me from my peaceful nap, and I too screamed, "AAAHHHHH!"

It took precisely one second to discern that everyone in the room was staring at me in disbelief.

"Is there a problem, Mr. Butterworth?" Dr. Floyd spoke slowly and deliberately.

"No sir, no problem at all."

But that wasn't true. The difference between 15 and 20 percent had created a problem, a big one that I didn't even know about. Once again, I had blown it. This time, it wasn't temper, it was slumber. Either way, I figured I was in deep yogurt.

I thought of calling Edmund to relate my latest blunder, but I figured he was still trying to coax Denise out of the ladies' room, so he wouldn't be near a phone.

My stomach churned as I thought of the mess I had created. *Well, on the brighter side, maybe all this stress at work will help me in my attempt to lose weight. Maybe I'll be thin enough to snag the perfect woman of my dreams at my reunion—the one who has no recollection of a fat kid named Butterworth.*

7

Being stuck in traffic is not all bad for me. I find that I need the extra time to change from my work person to my home person. I don't mean physically—I tried that once and did three thousand dollars' damage to my Honda and then had to give a policeman an accident report in my underwear.

No, I'm referring to the mental debriefing that a working person has to engage in before the home assault occurs. It's putting on the back burner my outburst in the department meeting, and realizing that worrying won't change anything. Tomorrow's another day. Tomorrow I'll cut 20 percent from my budget, be scolded by Dr. Floyd, face the fact of no raise this year, and go to class in order to communicate to my students the joys of teaching.

My favorite activity while waiting in a line of automobiles is people-watching. What do other people do while stuck in traffic on the way home from work?

For example, take the late-model tan Volvo that drove next to me for ten miles. It obviously carried the carpool from the office. Some kind of business discussion was going on, and it appeared to be a rather intense one. Neck veins bulged, an occasional fist pounded the leather-padded steering wheel, and reports waved high in the air offering further proof of particular positions.

Some people just don't know when to clock out.

Of course, as usual, one person had opted to forgo the discussion. I could tell this by the way he aimlessly gazed out the side window of the car, his expression silently screaming, "Isn't there a carjacker in the area who would be interested in a little action?"

I smiled and waved.

Another vehicle type I've spotted in growing numbers during the rush hour parade of brake lights is the mother-truck. Mother-truck drivers are usually known for their strength. Biceps bulging under their T-shirts (this applies to both male and female drivers), deeply tanned forearms hanging out the window, sunglasses in any kind of weather. Add or subtract the shotgun in the rear window gun rack based on your own state's laws governing the lifestyles of self-made cowboys and cowgirls.

On the other side of the driving spectrum is the corporate CEO in his or her top-of-the-line Mercedes or BMW. More than likely the car is painted black, deep blue, or dark green, which must be power colors. Two thousand dollars' worth of suit coat is hung by a cedar hanger on the hook by the window behind the driver's seat above the Corinthian leather interior. (Is Corinthian leather to be considered "carnal" to a Christian?) All windows are rolled up, no matter what weather condition, as the automatic climate control brings the perfect temperature of seventy-two degrees to our business champion, who is, naturally, wheeling and dealing on the car phone for the entire journey.

I always see a lot of the ubiquitous minivan, usually in white, silver, or the wood-paneled look. These are most often commandeered by young moms in semi-frazzled states. They have mastered the uncanny ability of never taking their eyes off the road in front of them while accomplishing seven to ten tasks in the seats directly behind them. While driving, these amazing females can:

—find the baby's pacifier

—readjust the toddler's car seat

—correct a spelling pretest

—open a plastic bottle of juice

—clean up a spilled bottle of juice

—consult a road map

—take a turn at Battleship

—tie the shoelaces of a soccer cleat

—peruse a document from the office

As I pulled into our driveway, I was focused on making something quick for dinner, since I promised Ben I'd help him prepare for his social studies exam. That's when the truth hit me, and hit me hard. Of all the cars I had passed that night, I had the most in common with the women in the minivans!

In caveman days men were known for fire, rocks, and eventually, the wheel. But around my house we're now known for tuna, microwave, and eventually, the fork. Something is deeply wrong with this picture.

I know a lot of men who like to cook. But don't tell me you like to cook if you're one of these weekend-barbecue-grill kind of guys. Tell me you like to cook in the middle of the winter, when it's just you and the casserole dish. If that turns you on, you need a jump from twelve thousand feet to slap you back to reality.

My sons were their usual helpful selves concerning dinner. They didn't actually *do* anything to help, but they offered a medley of encouraging cheers to get me through the cooking hour.

—When do we eat?

—Isn't it ready yet?

—We're not having that same old yucky Tuna Surprise again, are we?

—Dad, something stinks over by the stove!

—I just ate the last can of tuna in a sandwich, but, if I remember correctly, I think there is one more can out in the garage under the box of Christmas decorations.

—Shouldn't it be ready by now?

—The Johnsons eat a lot more healthy than we do, Dad. They say you're killing us.

—Are you causing the tuna fish to be put on the endangered species list?

—Don't let that stuff all over the inside of the microwave bother you, Dad. Bo just cooked a hot dog a few minutes extra and it kinda, sorta exploded.

Usually, my only friend on Tuna Surprise night is the cat. This used to bother me, but I noticed that when my dad came out to visit over Christmas, he cooked up a great meal of roast beef, potatoes with gravy, and he was met with the same response my tuna receives…"Is this all we're having for dinner?"

Living with four boys is a lot like running a fraternity house, minus the toga parties and John Belushi. The boys sit down to our dinner table, endure a prayer, keep their heads bowed, and concentrate intently on the food that sits before them on their plates. Attempting conversation is a little like drilling for oil…sometimes you get lucky, but mostly it's duds.

This night turned out to be no exception.

"Anything interesting happen in school today?" I ventured. Nothing but the sounds of chewing filled the air.

"Did you lift weights after school today, Brandon?"

"Hrrrummph." This is code for "Yes" with "Narrrrraphh" being its antonym for "No."

"How was your day, BJ?" I asked.

"My senior project is due in two weeks," he stated between bites. "Pass the lemonade, please."

"How far along are you?"

"Haven't started yet."

"When was it assigned?"

"Couple months ago."

"BJ..." My heart rate increased to where I feel like I *really* do have an oil derrick pumping inside my chest.

"Relax, Dad, it's cool."

Oh, to be young and ignorant again.

"Will you have it ready to turn in on time?" I asked, which was really a ridiculous question. Did I really think he'd reply, "No, Dad, I think I'm looking at an F." Does a kid ever warn you in advance that he has carefully planned to flunk?

"No problem."

I am consistently impressed with how teenagers can take large chunks of thought and reduce them to a verbal answer of two or three words. If teenagers ran the nightly news for Tom Brokaw, they could cover a thirty-minute report in about seven.

"What's happening in your world, Bo?" I once again shifted directional pursuits.

"Fine." (Notice how the answer doesn't fit the question.) "I need help on my spelling, Dad."

"He can't do it!" Ben interrupted calmly, yet defiantly. "He promised to help me with my social studies test. He has no time for you and your spelling words."

"Dad!" Bo cried out.

Ben smiled the smile that says, "Mission accomplished."

"Hey, hey, settle down," I interjected. "Ben, I will help you with your social studies, just like I promised. But I can also help Bo at the same time, right?"

Bo's smile said, *"Et tu, Brute!"*

Ben shook his head. "I don't like it, Dad. The last time you tried to help me with my homework *and* you tried to help Ben with something he was doing, I flunked."

All the boys put little smirks on their faces, each one recalling a time in the past where I have tried to do more than one thing at a time and made a mess of all of it. It's rough living with people who know you that well.

"Help me clear the table and load the dishwasher and we can get started," I instructed the boys after our four-minute meal. With these big eaters, it doesn't take long to polish off Tuna Surprise. The cat whined her disapproval over no leftovers, but we haven't had leftovers since November of 1987.

Ben handed me two tattered pieces of yellow paper, along with two pieces of white notebook paper, in equally trashed form. "The yellow papers are the questions and the notebook paper has the answers on them," he informed me as we moved from the kitchen to the warmth of the fire in the family room.

How can it be that a junior-higher can fold, spindle, and mutilate pieces of paper simply by moving them from the classroom to the home? Ben has given me permission slips to sign that look like early draft copies of the *Magna Carta.*

"And here are my spelling words," Bo added, handing me his fifth-grade spelling workbook.

"Okay, one at a time," I refereed. "Ben, let's start with you: How old must a person be in order to be a United States senator?"

Ben paused to think about this query. I know that when Ben pauses, he has no idea of the answer. If it's not right there at the tip of his cranium, it is lost somewhere in the lower abdomen.

"Wait—I know this one," Ben said, offering the classic stall line. "It's twenty-five, right? A person has to be twenty-five in order to be a U.S. senator."

"No, that's how old you have to be to be a *representative*. You have to be thirty to be a senator." As I corrected Ben, his eyes rolled, his lip curled, and he shrugged his shoulders.

"Okay...whatever..."

"How many representatives make up the House of Representatives?" I asked, prodding him right along.

"Four hundred thirty-five."

"Correct. How is the number of representatives that serve in the House decided?"

"By the rights of the government to purchase private property for public use which occurred before the law was made by Barbara Boxer and Dianne Feinstein."

I quickly scanned the questions on the yellow sheets and the answers on the white ones.

"That's a good answer, Ben. You defined for me *eminent domain*, as well as an *ex post facto law*, with the names of California's two senators thrown in for good measure. That's an excellent medley of civics data beautifully woven together."

"Thank you, Dad," Ben replied, beaming from ear to ear.

"Unfortunately," I continued, "it doesn't answer the question of how the number of representatives is decided."

"Okay...whatever..."

"Ben, the correct answer is that the representatives are determined by the population of each state."

"Good, good, that's good to know," Ben mused. I tried to tell by the expression on his face whether the piece of information had actually moved out of his abdominal cavity into a nice warm home in his brain.

"Hey, whattabout me?" Bo piped up. I had unwittingly committed the cardinal breech of tutorial etiquette by asking Ben *two* questions in a row without having Bo spell a word from his spelling list.

As I was about to utter his first word, the telephone rang. This is usually not an issue for me, since at home I get one call per one hundred calls to the boys. So, it was indeed an amazing announcement when Brandon yelled from his stereo-infested bedroom, "Dad, it's for you!"

Tossing all decorum (and homework) aside, I sprung to the phone like a man possessed. "Hello?" I gushed. My mind was spinning. *If someone is calling me, it must be important, I thought. Maybe it's the president of the community college calling for some advice, or the governor or maybe even the president of the United States!*

"Hi, Bill, it's me, Edmund."

"Oh, hi Edmund," I said, trying to maintain the same expectant air in my voice, so he wouldn't know I was disappointed it was only him and not the governor.

"I forgot to tell you on the phone earlier today that your appointment with Dr. Graydon is on Wednesday morning at eight-thirty. I figured that would give you enough time to drive over to the campus and make your ten-thirty class."

"You're a thoughtful guy, Edmund," I replied, still unsure of the whole physical exam issue. I would say I was getting cold feet, but the real truth is there were never warm toes.

"My appointment's at ten, so I know you'll get out of there in time to drive over to your class." Boy, was Edmund naive. When was the last time you were in any kind of doctor's office that kept its appointments on time?

Ben and Bo were both over by the phone by now, sighing, methodically crossing their arms and then uncrossing them, pointing to their little eight-dollar digital watches and making me feel like the biggest creep in the world for actually having a friend.

"Edmund, I'm going to have to run here in a second. I'm quizzing a couple of the boys on their homework and they're getting impatient waiting for me."

"Okay, I understand," Edmund replied. "I'm proud of you for pitching in and helping the boys with their studies. It sounds like you're getting your life together, my man."

"Thanks, Edmund. I don't know what I'd do without you being in my corner."

"My pleasure. Oh, there's one more thing the doctor's office wanted me to tell you," he continued.

"What's that?"

"Welllll…" Edmund was stalling, not a good sign.

"What is it, Edmund?" I pushed him.

"After you eat dinner on Tuesday night, you're not allowed to have anything to eat until your physical is over on Wednesday. You know, fasting, for the blood test."

"That shouldn't be a problem," I replied casually.

"Well actually, you can't have anything to eat or *drink*, Bill. Just water." He paused to let that sink in. Just in case it didn't, he spelled it out for me.

"That means no coffee, either."

"No coffee?" Suddenly the phone receiver crashed to the floor as my arm went limp. I picked it back up and started rambling incoherently to Edmund.

"HowamIgonnagetallthewaytoeightthirtyinthemorningwithoutastrongcupofcoffee? WhodotheythinkIamsomesortofsuperhumanbeing? Thisisanoutrage!"

"DAAAADDDD!" By now the boys were coming unglued in their quest to wait patiently for the old man.

"Sounds like you gotta go," Edmund said quickly. "Talk to ya tomorrow. Bye."

Now I was shaken to my very foundation. No one ever said getting your life together would require a moratorium on coffee. Cotton-mouthed and sweaty-palmed, I returned to my task of helping to educate my children.

Their notes were still on the floor where I had dropped them when the phone rang. I picked them up and turned to the book that contained Bo's spelling list. This week he was studying words that end in -ery. "Bo, can you spell discovery?"

"D-I-S-C-O-V-E-R-Y, discovery," he rattled off in proper military precision.

"That's correct," I said.

"Dad," he said in that matter-of-fact tone that is so adult for a ten-year-old, "don't you remember? Spelling is my favorite subject. I always do well in it."

"Hit me with another question, Dad," Ben interjected. His competitive junior-high juices were flowing now that Bo had made himself out to be Mr. Spelling.

Why must everything be a contest with kids? Who can eat the most? Who can eat the fastest? Who can listen to his music the loudest? Who can stay up the latest? Who can sleep through his alarm the longest? Who can make the grossest sound? Who can go the longest time without a shower?

"Who would become president if both the president and the vice president were unable to serve?"

Ben's eyes lit up as it was clear I hit on a question which he could answer.

"Speaker of the House," he rattled off with the nonchalance of a secret agent. He turned and smiled at Bo.

"That's right," I smiled. "Bo, spell cemetery."

"C-E-M-E-T-E-R-Y, cemetery." Bo smiled back at Ben, and we stood at deuce.

"Dad, do you know anything about parallelograms?" Brandon screamed out of his decibel-defying room of noise.

"Where must all revenue bills begin?"

"In the House."

"That's correct. Spell misery. No, I don't, Brandon."

"M-I-S-E-R—"

"Dad, can I borrow twenty bucks?" It was BJ, totally oblivious to the study hall that was taking place. Ben and Bo looked up at him with a mixture of anger and disgust.

"Are you 100 percent sure you don't know *anything* about parallelograms, Dad?"

"M-I-S—"

"No, it's my turn," Ben interrupted.

"Twenty? Till Saturday?"

"EVERYBODY BEEEE QUUUUIIIIIEEEETTTTT!" I screamed with the force of a scud missile. I had tried bravely to stay calm as the world around me collapsed, but, alas, as the great philosopher Popeye would say with that squint in his eye, "I knows what I can stands and I can't stands no more!"

Except that instead of sounding like Popeye, I came off as Bluto, the big bully. BJ knew what was coming, so he spun on the heels of his work boots and made a mad dash for his car. Brandon must have guessed as well, for the sounds of his disco inferno were suddenly muffled by the closing of his door quietly behind him. Ben, upon the realization that he was stuck in the same room with me, leaned forward on the couch, and put his head in his hands like a man carrying the weight of the world on his shoulders. And poor Bo. God bless him, he was still young enough to have his eyes well up with tears.

And that left me, the new man, the changed person, the guy who was going to get his life together, sitting in the Naugahyde recliner...

No words were exchanged for a few moments, but Bo and Ben had apparently been communicating nonverbally. They both came over to the imitation-leather recliner that held my weary frame. One son on either side, they each put an arm around me, and Bo said, "It's okay, Dad. We all lose our cool."

"Thanks for helping me with my social studies, Dad," Ben added softly.

"Yeah, thanks for helping me with my spelling words," Bo also joined in.

With that, they quietly moved out of the family room, leaving me alone with the fireplace and my thoughts.

That night my thoughts centered around how easy it is for me to blow it. I had dozens of examples from that one day alone. But how grateful I was to have such understanding, forgiving children. They could've made it rough on me, but they chose to thank me for the little I did contribute. I offered up a small prayer of thanks to the Lord. Before long, the fire's glow was faded and it was time to tuck everyone in for the night.

By the time I wandered back to the bedrooms, Bo was already in his pajamas, about to fall asleep in his bed. But he looked up from his spelling words, seeming very proud of what he was about to do as he said to me:

"Daddy, I love you. And that is not just F-L-A-T-T-E-R-Y, flattery!"

hen I climbed out of bed on Wednesday morning, I was met with a cold, dark rain. It was a sign from God. "Yes, my son, this is the sort of day I have created with you in mind. It is the perfect morning for a man to go without coffee and to visit his doctor. This is my gift to you, my child, and I am well pleased."

I wasn't.

My boys each took a turn at joking with me about my day at the doctor's, but when a man hasn't had his morning coffee, even Bob Hope isn't funny.

I really should have left the house early to get some work done over at the college before I drove to Dr. Graydon's, but, as so often happens, it took me a long time to get out of the house that morning. So, I grudgingly turned the wheel of the Accord toward downtown Pine Woods, where I imagined Dr. Graydon awaited with glee.

As I cruised down the main road in our little town, it was also obvious that we were all listening to the same radio station. When the morning disc-jockey informed us of a fender-bender blocking traffic on the road that leads to the center of town, all of our brake lights went on at the same time. The brave drivers looked for a spot to U-turn, as well as for cops who might ticket such illegal maneuvering.

I do not like to live dangerously, so a U-turn was out of the question for me. Sure enough, the speeds decreased and we approached town at about fifteen miles per hour. I glanced nervously at my watch, remembering that I was supposed to be there fifteen minutes early to fill out forms since I hadn't visited the doctor for awhile.

In an attempt to take my mind off the inevitable, I started fiddling with the car radio. Like most cars, my Honda has six buttons that allow you to preset your radio station preferences. Living in a democracy, that meant each of my four boys had a button that was all theirs, and I took charge of the remaining two in a bloodless coup.

BJ owned the first button, and as I hit it, I was immediately sorry. It was the local all-rap station.

Brandon, the guru of seventies disco, had the second button set to an oldies station that plays just that decade. This music made me think about purchasing my first leisure suit on a warm summer's day in 1976...

I walked in wearing tennis shoes but had to change into a pair of three-inch platform shoes for the tailoring of the pants. It was part of the look to have hems that dropped forty-five degrees from the front to the back so as to hug your platforms. I am a loyal guy, so I still have that leisure suit in the back of my closet.

Each of my boys has taken a turn wearing it, too, and every time they got more candy that Halloween than any other.

I shook my head and turned to the third button on the radio. This is Ben's choice and it's another oldies station, but plays songs from the fifties and the sixties. I left it there for a minute as the Temptations finished up "Ain't Too Proud to Beg." I remembered lying awake in bed at night listening to that song in high school, wondering if I should tell Sherry Rich or Ruth Jensen how I really felt about her. "Should I beg?" I would ask myself.

Then it hit me. What if I saw them at the reunion and they weren't married? This could be the chance I have waited for twenty-five years! *Yikes,* I thought. *I've got to drop some weight and get it together. Good thing that's where I'm headed. Onward to Doc's!*

Next, Frankie Valli and the Four Seasons started singing "Let's Hang On." This was a good time in our history. There we had a grown man singing in a falsetto that made him sound like a girl. But no one complained or questioned his orientation. It was all right with America, and we bought his records by the millions. (I always thought it would be fun to have Neil Sedaka and Anne Murray sing a duet—Neil could sing the girl's part and Anne could sing the boy's. I bet it would sell...)

Button number four is Bo's domain, a Hispanic station that broadcasts entirely in Spanish. He enjoys the disc jockeys who are passionate about their weather forecasts, and the music that's heavy on castanets. He even has his clock radio at home set to this station, and he sets his alarm each night in gleeful anticipation of *mañana.*

The last two buttons are mine. One button is the twenty-four-hour news station, a radio version of CNN. But I must have been drifting in and out. I heard that Boris Yeltsin had signed a five-year contract to coach the New England Patriots and the movie critic gave it four stars.

The final button is the local Christian radio station. It was time for *Focus on the Family,* the Godfather of Christian radio broadcasting. Mike was introducing tomorrow's program, which meant the show was almost over, and that it must be eight-thirty, and I was already late for my appointment with destiny.

Fortunately, the medical building was now visible. I pulled into the parking lot, sighing with relief that there were all sorts of parking spaces available. But as I moved closer, I discovered that all those spots were reserved for doctors, medical personnel, the handicapped, and emergency vehicles. I wasn't A, B, C, or D. So I had to be E—none of the above. I headed the car back out to Main Street.

There are plenty of parking lots in our little town, and just like a page from a Norman Rockwell book, each lot has the warm, inviting sign over it:

Customer Parking Only
All Others Will Be Towed
Have A Nice Day

The first parking space I located that I could park in without fear of prosecution was at a Denny's restaurant. I hustled out of my car and ran as fast as my legs would carry me to Dr. Graydon's office.

It's not a good move to burst into a doctor's office with face flushed, wheezing, tears in your eyes, and leg muscles twitching because they just received more exercise in the last three minutes than they have since 1969.

"Hi, I'm Bill Butterworth and I'm here for my eight-thirty appointment with Dr. Graydon!" I said this as suavely as is possible while experiencing cardiac arrest.

"It's eight-forty. You're late," the receptionist barked.

"Sorry," I replied meekly.

"Fill these out," she said, jamming a clipboard under my nose. It was packed with forms, the kind of forms with lots of tiny spaces for the purpose of recording when you had your distemper booster, the number of times you ever had the flu, and how you managed to fall out of a wagon when you were five.

I can't get even the simplest of the health insurance information correct. I know mine has a logo with some sort of colored cross, and I think it's blue or red but I get them mixed up. I know one of them is run by Elizabeth Dole and they will give you free blankets if your house floats away in a flood. But I think the other one is run by Saddam Hussein and he will just laugh if you dare think that his company would pay for any of the medical services you require.

When I bought the Blue/Red/Whatever Cross health insurance, the only way I could afford the monthly payments was to get a deductible equal to the national debt. I'll be paying for most medical procedures well into my nineties. But it's comforting to know I'm protected from the two unheard-of life-threatening diseases the plan would cover in full.

I finished filling out the insurance information forms, which were on hot-pink paper, and turned my attention to the family medical history forms, printed on the goldenrod paper stock. This was going to get interesting. They wanted to know much more than I knew about my father, mother, grandfathers, and grandmothers.

I was brought up to be respectful, after all. If I had asked my grandmother about her pancreatic condition, I would have been soundly paddled on the behind and sent to my room for a week without meals.

I skimmed over the questions about my family tree and discovered that the doctor had all sorts of personal questions about *me*, too. I had to answer questions about cancer, heart disease, AIDS, diabetes, high blood pressure, headaches, prostate trouble, cataracts, hearing loss, incontinence, and unsightly warts and blemishes. About ten pages into the History of Butterworth Health, I turned to what looked like the last page. Only three more questions!

Do you smoke? I wrote the word "NO" in big letters, feeling a surge of good health.

Do you drink alcoholic beverages? Again, I wrote "NO," almost sensing the healthy blood coursing through my veins.

Do you drink coffee? I must admit, I stared at that one for quite some time before concluding the best thing to do in this instance was to be brave. So I left it blank.

It wasn't until that point that I glanced at my watch. It was nine-ten! I had been filling out forms for half an hour. If things didn't get hoppin' here, I was going to be lucky to get in before Edmund's ten o'clock appointment!

At that precise moment a door opened, revealing a large woman with gray hair and brown eyes surrounded by deep black circles. This woman hadn't slept since Lawrence Welk stopped selling Sominex. She was dressed completely in white, holding a Plexiglass clipboard with a single sheet of seaweed green paper on it. She had a stethoscope wrapped around her neck like a security blanket and a nameplate on her blouse that made her either a nurse or a local realtor.

"Mr. Butterworth?" she asked, looking around the waiting room to see who would respond. Since I was the only person in the waiting room, I felt sorry for her and said, "That's me."

"Fine. Are we through filling out our forms? Good. Let's move into Exam Room Fourteen and I'll obtain some additional information from you before Dr. Graydon sees you."

Obviously she expected me to jump, for she was already heading for Exam Room Fourteen while I was still in the process of collecting the history of my liver.

"By the way, my name is Sandy." She added her name as an afterthought, I felt. It was part of the drill, and I sensed she had done this a thousand times before.

"Step on the scale, Mr. Butterworth," Sandy demanded.

"Can I take my shoes off first?" I asked. What a day to wear one of my heavy sweaters! I could have kicked myself for not leaving my ring of keys in the car.

"That won't be necessary. Just step on the scale." Sandy had the empathy of a prison warden.

I reluctantly moved onto the scale as Sandy kept sliding all the moving hardware further and further to the right side of the scale. I waited for her to make a crack about how my next weigh-in would have to take place down on the docks. But she only grunted as she recorded the large number.

She then measured my height (I felt I had good height) and took my temperature (orally, thankfully). Next was the blood-pressure reading. I learned then that when a health professional is holding your wrist and checking her wristwatch, it's not a good time to ask her if she ever loses count.

The last item on Sandy's agenda was to have me look out the window at the rainy morning. As I turned my head to watch the showers, I could have sworn I felt the unmistakable prick of a needle piercing me. By the time I turned back it was too late. Sandy had a test tube filled with blood, placed neatly in a cool-looking metal rack full of other tubes of blood. I didn't have the stomach to see if my name was on more than one tube.

"Thank you, Mr. Butterworth." Sandy stood up and delivered her exit line. "Dr. Graydon will be with you shortly."

I tried to smile, but could only manage to appear faint and nauseous.

"Are you all right?" Sandy asked. She seemed concerned about my health, probably because it was throwing her off schedule.

"I'm okay." I responded weakly. That was good enough for Sandy. As she closed the exam-room door, she left one more set of instructions for me.

"Go ahead and strip to your underwear, and Dr. Graydon will be right here."

She closed the door quietly behind her, sensing my need for privacy. It was thoughtful of her to respect my modesty, and I made a point of telling her so when she popped her head back in just after I had removed my pants.

Alone and almost naked, I stared around the room that had given birth to the term *sterile*. There were boxes of tissues, jars of tongue depressors, cans of ear inspectors, tubes of jelly, and, of course, small rectangular cardboard containers that had words printed on the sides "Slip-resistant Exam Gloves." Just my luck, not only were there one hundred in a box, but the side of the box also indicated that they came in three sizes: S, M, and L. Dr. Graydon's glove of choice was L, which I guess stood for Lucky Me.

I heard someone jiggling the doorknob of my exam room. I didn't know if it was Dr. Graydon or Sandy coming by for another free peek. I breathed a little easier when the man of the hour waltzed into the room.

"Well, well, well, if it isn't Bill Butterworth," Dr. Graydon gushed. "I'm going to have to check my chart to figure out the last time I've seen you in here. It's been quite some time, hasn't it?"

I didn't have the courage to tell him our last visit could be best measured in decades, so I did my best to change the subject. "Doc, don't give me a hard time now—you remember, I was in here last month with Brandon! Those stitches you put in healed up quite nicely. You do good work!"

Dr. Graydon beamed. "He's a good boy, that Brandon—and one fine football player, too." Dr. Graydon was the volunteer team doctor for Brandon's football team, so he knew what he was talking about. I swelled my naked chest in pride over his compliments of my son.

Dr. Graydon was standing in front of me staring at his clipboard as I gave him a once-over. I put him at about five-foot-seven, brown hair, a small mustache, and the start of a receding hairline. His long, white lab coat had his name embroidered over the left chest pocket. Under his lab coat, he was wearing a faded green golf shirt, blue jeans, and a pair of black high-top Reebok pumps.

"So how are we feeling these days?" the doctor began.

"I'm okay, Doc," I responded without a second's hesitation. "It just felt like it was time for a physical, so here I am."

"Yes, I see. Your friend Edmund Holmes called and made an appointment for both of you, isn't that correct?"

"Uh, yes, sir," I answered.

"Edmund's an old friend of mine," Dr. Graydon smiled. "As a matter of fact, he's my accountant."

"That's nice," I offered.

"He was telling me that the two of you attended some sort of weekend men's retreat and you both felt like you needed to make some changes in your physical regimen. Is that correct?"

Leave it to good ol' Edmund to brief the doctor on my life's goals before I even get in the office. Suddenly I felt like the doctor knew more about me than he should. But I was stuck. He was standing between me and my pants.

"Uhh, yeah, kinda," I was now answering him as if I had regressed to thirteen years of age.

"Well, I can tell you right off, you need to lose some weight."

"Really?" I said, acting as surprised as I could.

"Yes, definitely. Tell me about your weekly schedule of exercise," he commanded. He started systematically thunking me with a little hammer to test my reflexes.

"There's not much to tell," I confessed as my leg kicked like a Rockette's.

"I see," the doctor said in the same tone of voice Ward Cleaver used to use when the Beaver admitted to cheating on Miss Lander's English compositions.

We were quiet for a minute as he listened to the front of me and the back of me through his stethoscope.

"Bill, you might want to think about joining a health club or jogging or playing racquetball or *something*." He said "something" the way he might say, "Do something or you'll be dead by Friday."

"Tell me about your diet," he continued.

"There's not much to say, really," I stumbled.

"How's that?" he raised his eyebrows.

It was futile to try to fake him out. It was time to come clean.

"Basically whatever food is bad for you I tend to eat in excess."

"That's got to change, Bill."

"I know," I barely whispered.

"When you leave today, the receptionist can give you some brochures on proper diet, healthy exercise programs, and we even have some discount coupons for a couple of the local health clubs. Make sure you grab some, okay?"

"Okay."

"We'll have a more precise profile of your health once we get the results from the blood work back from the lab. That normally takes a few days, so it should be early next week when we'll have a more complete picture. I'll have one of the nurses give you a call when the test results are in."

I nodded in agreement. As Dr. Graydon looked at me, he seemed to understand my fears. He reached out to put his hand on my shoulder and said, "Relax, Bill. You're just fine. You have all you need to get yourself together. I'm confident that you can do it."

I wished I shared his confidence. This was going to be tough, and no one knew it better than I did. But I was deeply appreciative of Dr. Graydon's sensitivity.

I was about to thank him for his kindness when he said one last thing, holding up a newly gloved hand: "Oh, yes, before I forget, *please bend over.*"

9

By the time I recovered enough to stand up straight, get dressed, and walk stiffly to the receptionist's desk for my brochures, it was ten forty-five. By now my classroom was empty and twenty-three students in twenty-three different parts of the campus were giving thanks to God.

As soon as I opened the door to the waiting room, I saw Edmund nervously paging through a *Good Housekeeping* from 1989. I surmised that he had already perused the older material and was now trying to calm his nerves by learning *Thirty Ways to Wow Your Family with Yellow Squash.*

"How'd it go?" Edmund asked, concerned for his own survival.

"I can't tell you," I lied. "The doctor made me promise I wouldn't say anything to you."

He started to perspire freely, quite a sight on a rainy winter's day.

"Look at me, I'm sweating!" Edmund said in exasperation.

"Well," I replied. "It's going to take more than sweat to get us back in shape. Call me when you're through here and I'll meet you for lunch over at the grocery store. I suggest we meet at the produce aisle. We'll both eat a radish."

Edmund was in no condition to eat a relaxing lunch after his visit with the doctor, so I rejoiced alone that Dr. Graydon had neglected to bring up the issue of coffee. I drove over to the local gourmet coffee shop (clearly a knock-off of Starbucks) and ordered a grande latte with a double shot of espresso. Soon the caffeine would return me to life.

While they were preparing my drink, I wandered over to the pay phone on the back wall to call my voice mail at the college. I wondered if there would be a nasty message from Dr. Floyd. I was willing to bet he'd already heard that I missed my class, and now he'd want to see me in his office.

The thought was enough to tempt me to hang up before the call went through. But in light of my newfound efforts to get my life together, I decided to be brave, stay on the line, and face the music. The electronic lady told me I had only one message, so I braced myself for Dr. Floyd's perfectly enunciated whine.

"Hi Bill! It's Tom Graham!" Tom's voice was upbeat and lively, resembling the third-base coach who had flagged him on into home plate so many times in his ball-playing days.

"Bill, when you have a minute, I'd like you to call me back, if you would. Based on some of the things we learned at Kenny Kramer's weekend men's retreat, I'm attempting to put together a small group of guys that would meet weekly to talk together, pray together, and basically, just be accountable to one another. I immediately thought of you and Edmund, so I'm giving him a call also.

"We're planning a little introductory meeting tomorrow morning at six over at the Pine Woods Cafe. I really hope you'll consider it, Bill. Personally, I'd love to have you as a part of our group. Well, this message is getting a little long, so I better quit before I use up all your tape. Like I said, call me and hopefully I'll see you in the morning. God bless you, brother!"

The electronic lady announced in that sultry tone of hers, "No...

more…messages…" and I hung up the phone. *I wish she were real,* I thought, *I'd ask her out!*

By now my latte was ready. I paid my money and found an empty table by the window where I could sit, nurse my drink, and be alone with my thoughts…

The morning's rain had stopped, and the slickness on the streets gave our little town the look of an old black-and-white fifties movie. I imagined Humphrey Bogart striding by in a trench coat in one of those cool hats they used to wear.

Guys can't get away with wearing broad-brimmed fedoras anymore, unless you're a private investigator. Occasionally, out on the golf course, you'll catch a man in a tan or white, straw-hat version (and he'll usually claim his doctor is making him wear it for medical reasons—avoiding skin cancer on the forehead and earlobes). But for the average male in the United States of America in the 1990s there is one and only one acceptable form of headgear and that is *the Baseball Cap.*

I know all the cowboys will take exception with me here, but again, I'm talking the broad population which utilizes headgear for a day at the beach, a sold-out grandstand at Wrigley Field, and an afternoon in Central Park. Face it, cowboys, the world is bigger than a stroll down the main street in Amarillo.

Yes, it's the baseball cap that captures the imagination of young and old alike. Starting with the genuine insignias of the current major league teams, ball caps have expanded into a billion-dollar business with endless choices:

—*Nostalgia ball caps* Now you can wear the same logos as the 1952 Philadelphia Phillies or the 1948 Brooklyn Dodgers or the '27 Yankees. That's right, the same cap the Bambino, the Iron Horse, and Miller Huggins wore! These caps are especially popular with aging baby boomers and their toothless fathers.

—*Entertainment logos* Now everyone can wear a cap with the logo of Warner Brothers, Universal Studios, or even your favorite movie or TV show. Back when I was growing up, who would have dared to ride the school bus in a new *Dick Van Dyke Show* cap or that snazzy *Son of Flubber* number? Wearing caps like those, we could have rocked our world.

—*Logos for every sport imaginable* Is it only me, or is there a conflict of terms in wearing a *baseball* cap with a logo from the National *Basketball* Association? Would these people ever consider wearing a football helmet with the insignia of the Cleveland Indians on it? (Although with all Cleveland's been through with the Browns, they just might.)

—*Christian ball caps* Apparently ball caps can have a conversion experience, for there are Christian hats out there in the world, arguably being salt and light to the otherwise heathen world of headgear. Caps say everything from "Jesus" to "First Baptist" to "The 700 Club" to "C.S. Lewis Fan Club."

Sipping my latte at the front of the coffee shop, my mind moved from ball caps to the men that wear them. I wondered whom Tom invited to be part of this group he was forming. Was Edmund invited to make me feel comfortable, meaning everyone else would make me feel uncomfortable? Was this going to be one of these nineties-guy things, a holdover from the sensitivity sessions of the sixties? Were we all going to be asked to sit on blankets, assume the fetal position, and recall our feelings in the womb and other mother-related psychoses?

I knew if I gave this thing a chance, it would most likely be a good experience for me. I needed people in my life who would love me and care about me and hold me accountable. Kenny Kramer was crystal-clear on the importance of groups of this nature in *Getting It Together*

Mentally and Emotionally and its follow-up session, *Getting It Together Spiritually*.

Plus, it would be good to be influenced by a guy like Tom Graham. I never really said it in so many words, but I idolized this guy. He loved the Lord, had a great family, and had a pipeline to the Dodger front office. Here was a man who truly earned the right to wear a ball cap.

Being the rugged individualist that I am, I decided to consider my decision about joining this group for the rest of the day, and then later that evening call Edmund and let him decide for the both of us.

Edmund's spin on being invited to Tom's group was that it was "an answer to prayer." So with my mind made up for me, I awoke the next morning to the sound of my clock radio at five o'clock. Bo had reset my dial, so I was greeted by a mariachi band and a weather report of *muy frio*. I took that to mean "very cold" or "more beans."

I stumbled to the bathroom and immediately turned on the shower, knowing at this hour of the morning, at this freezing outdoor temperature, I might not have hot water before the next session of Congress convened. Hot water is in abundant supply in our hot-water heater, if you only count August. Otherwise, it takes forever to get a temperature that's even close to lukewarm.

(As a Christian, I've always been fascinated by that term *lukewarm*. Do you think it had its roots back in the four Gospels? If so, why isn't it *matthewwarm*, *markwarm*, or *johnwarm*? Perhaps it is Luke's medical background that gives him the edge in this naming of a standard for the measurement of a given liquid's temperature.)

The shower was freezing, but the clock was moving, so I jumped into a stall not fit for Judas Iscariot. In a fury, I lathered, rinsed, and was out before one number had changed on my digital clock. I was cold, but clean.

Gazing into the bathroom mirror, I rubbed my hand over my face to check the shaving decision. In God's rich goodness and grace, he has made me blonde and fair, so I generally shave once every two months whether I need it or not. I pity those same guys I envied in junior high.

Remember those guys who were already shaving in sixth grade? Growing up with a lot of Italian friends, I saw these guys get fuzzy chins while most of us were still on pacifiers. I wonder what some of these same guys will look like at the reunion. Have they grown hair in even more places, and will they remember to bring their razors? Maybe, merely by comparison, I won't look so bad after all.

I shivered as I ran over to my closet in order to pick out something warm and flattering to wear for my first impression on the men's group. As is true for most overweight men, the clothes closet is a visit to skinny days gone by. Approximately 88 to 94 percent of the clothes in this closet are too small, the margin of error based on the previous evening's intake of ice cream, chips and salsa, or Tastykakes.

This was particularly distressing this morning, as I wanted to make a good impression. The only clothes that seemed to fit were my old comfortable sweatshirts. Those sorts of finery don't scream "class," "character," or "distinction."

In desperation I put on a handsome, long-sleeved dress shirt I bought a couple of years ago, but alas, the buttons would not agree to meet with the buttonholes in the neutral zone of the stomach area. I tossed up my hands in disgust and threw a navy blue sweatshirt over my head. I vowed again to lose weight while also wondering if Tom would bring Danish and/or donuts to the meeting.

The idea of leaving my boys on their own to get off to school brought another form of shivering to my body. "They'll be just fine," I reassured myself. I jogged over to the kitchen, made a quick jumbo cup of coffee, closed the door quietly behind me, jumped in the Honda, cranked it up (over and over on a cold morning like this one), and threw it into gear.

Driving down my driveway, I realized the last radio station I listened to yesterday was the Christian station and the lucky guy who preaches on the airwaves at five-thirty in the morning was in full gear. I'm not familiar with this gentleman, but his accent led me to believe that he must be one of these mega-church pastors from Texas or Mississippi who takes his sermon tapes and turns them into radio shows. Subtle hints gave this away, like the little girl who had the whooping cough attack in the front pew of the sanctuary and her parents didn't believe she should be excused from church, so she hacked through the whole message, much to the dismay of radio listeners.

This guy was preaching from the book of Haggai. He was a real go-getter, too. In my mind's eye I could see him frothing at the mouth. Suddenly it dawned on me as he was preaching that I am totally unfamiliar with the words of Haggai. The guy could be making all of it up, for all I knew. Not having a Bible in front of me, I was trusting that this guy wasn't some charlatan who makes Haggai say whatever he wants it to. I made a mental note to read Haggai when I got home that night, but somehow I already knew it would be one of those mental notes whose stickum fails and it falls off the refrigerator door to an early death.

As I pulled up to Pine Woods Cafe I recognized Tom's baby blue '67 Mustang convertible parked in front. The car is in immaculate shape, befitting the perfect man. Next to it was Edmund's jet black Lexus ES 300. This is the only sore point in our friendship, as I am jealous beyond belief of Edmund's car. It's got a car phone and a CD player and automatic temperature control and tan leather interior and those sporty chrome/gold wheel covers and gold hood and trunk ornaments. Every time I see it, I remind myself that I should recheck to see how much Edmund charges me for his accounting services.

None of the other cars in the lot rang any bells in my mind, so I parked my Accord in the spot closest to the door and made a dash for the covering of the restaurant's awning. It was only sprinkling, but as a wearer of eye-glasses, I firmly believe if there is only one drop of moisture in the air, it will fall on one of my lenses, creating one of life's little irritations that can get so intense, you may end up buying a gun.

Once in the restaurant, I saw Tom in a cozy little booth in the back of the establishment wearing a beautiful blue warm-up suit. Seated next to Tom was Edmund, dressed in the uniform of a CPA: blue button-down Oxford dress shirt with a burgundy and gold rep stripe necktie.

Feeling self-conscious in my sweatshirt, I sighed in relief as I recognized the other guys seated next to Edmund. Greg Freeman is a local construction worker who spends half his year building homes for the very rich and the other half replacing redwood decks and small add-ons for the rest of us who don't possess big bucks. Greg is fun-loving and very savvy. He always laughs at my jokes.

Seated next to Greg was Nathan Johnstone, vice president of our local bank. He sat in perfect posture, his coiffed hair carefully sprayed into place. He wore a handsome gray pinstripe suit, a heavily starched shirt as white as light, accented by a solid-blue silk necktie with tiny gold crosses on it.

Now I was really nervous about how I looked, so my eye hastened back to Greg, who was wearing an old green-and-white flannel shirt with all sorts of paint flecks dotting it, along with a pair of beat-up jeans and work boots.

Thank you, Lord, for Greg, I silently prayed.

I slipped into the only remaining seat in the booth, between Nathan and Tom. The waitress came up behind me, her coffee pot dancing the dance of joy as she poured me a cup. No one seemed to be eating anything, unless you count *Sweet n' Low.* We all had coffee in front of us, except Tom, who was just about through drinking a large glass of orange juice.

"Have we already ordered?" I opened my menu and smiled, attempting some men's group pre-6 A.M. humor.

"Yes, we have, Bill," Tom answered in complete seriousness, oblivious to my joke, as were all the other men. "We decided it would help us concentrate better on matters at hand if we just had coffee or juice without the hassle of a meal."

"Good idea," I falsely forced out of a mouth. But I was thinking, *Maybe a warm oversized cinnamon bun dripping with melted butter and a side of bacon.*

"Well, let's talk about why we're here," Tom began. He pulled out a small, black-leather notebook and flipped to his prepared notes for this morning. "We were all at the retreat last weekend, and while meeting together as a group of guys is not something we would naturally do..."

My mind wandered at that point. Tom was right that men wouldn't naturally do this. Now a group of women...that's quite a different story. It seemed to me that in those rare moments when a woman is alone, she is actually only between small group meetings, in the car on the way, or walking from one group to another.

Women seem to do everything in groups, and their entire lives are spent systematically sharing their feelings with these groups. Men, on the other hand, in rare instances of sharing, always have to offer little disclaimers like, "In order to understand what I'm going through, I guess I need to give you a little bit of background...I guess I should start back in 1959...."

Meanwhile Tom was still working through the bullet points he had written on his notebook page. "I was thinking, perhaps it would be a good idea if we worked through a good book together. Reading a chapter at a time, we could meet together each week and discuss the salient points gleaned in our reading."

Reading? A *whole* book? Men? Something was wrong with this picture, but I couldn't quite put my finger on it.

"So what I'd like you to do for next week," Tom continued, "is to bring a list of books you'd like us to consider reading as a group. I think everyone should be able to bring in at least six titles."

Six book titles? I thought in the midst of a mild panic attack. *I'm going to have to go all the way back to junior high to come up with that many titles. I wonder if the guys will get suspicious if I suggest books like* Animal Farm *and* The Scarlet Letter. (I still have the *Cliff's Notes* for both of them.)

Then, in a burst of inspiration, it came to me: *I'll use the titles of six of my speech textbooks, claiming that we all need to bone up on our public speaking skills if we're going to share together.*

Tom continued. "I know in my life I have been blessed to read a lot of wonderfully inspirational books. Some have been so good, I have used them in my morning Quiet Time."

Quiet Time? I thought. This was the wrong time of year for me to have any personal time to read my Bible and pray. After all, it wasn't the first week of January. That's about the only time I can discipline myself enough to engage in that sort of activity. I had one more reason to be envious of Tom.

And he wasn't finished. "I also think it would be a good idea if we each came prepared next week to tell the rest of the group our life stories from the beginning up to the present."

I swallowed hard.

"You can chart it out for us, or bring in pictures, or just talk. But we want to know who you are, who you *really* are, as a result of this exercise. We probably won't get to everyone next week, but let's all come prepared, okay?"

My eyes darted around the table to observe that everyone seemed to think this was just great! Was I the only one who would develop an ulcer over this assignment?

I put on the same excited smile as my groupmates.

Once I smiled, I now had the hope that the other guys were wearing the same kind of smile—warm and *fake*. Fortunately, I could grill Edmund about this later. Maybe he'd be willing to write up my life story.

"That's all I had on my agenda," Tom concluded as I looked at my watch for the first time since arriving. Old Tom talked the whole hour away! I was amazed.

"Except I do have one more thing," he hastened to add. "I thought it would be good to go around the table and share prayer requests with each other."

Again my eyes moved side-to-side with warp speed. Everyone else seemed comfortable with one more way to be vulnerable with each other. "I'll start," Nathan began. "Please pray for me, as I have to make some important business decisions in the next few weeks. They are decisions that will have a fairly major effect on my career. It's safe to say it's pretty serious."

Most of the guys were writing down Nathan's request and I realized I had no writing implements. Had I found one, I could have scribbled the requests on a napkin or place mat.

"Pray for me and my wife," Greg followed. "As we get to know each other better I will share more, but if we're going to be accountable to each other, I need to tell you, we're struggling right now. We're not ready to split up or anything like that, but we really do need prayers, okay? We're seeing a counselor and it seems to be helping, but I know it's only God who can make this work."

"I'll go next," Tom said. "Pray for one of my daughters, Katie. She's having a tough time in graduate school right now and I know she'd appreciate your prayers."

Finally, it was between Edmund and me. I searched in vain under the table for his shin to kick, but it was nowhere to be found. Sensing my pain, Edmund spoke up.

"Bill and I are here for some very similar reasons. We both became incredibly convicted this past weekend. We stood to our feet to commit ourselves to getting our lives together physically, emotionally, and spiritually. I know I speak for both of us, don't I, Bill?"

I nodded my agreement.

"Like I said, I know I speak for both of us when I say we've both done a pretty good job of blowing it already. I've messed up and Bill has told me stories that would curl your hair!"

Why had I allowed Edmund to speak for me? I was just about to speak in my own defense when Edmund looked my way, smiled broadly and continued.

"Guys, Bill is my best friend, and I want him to succeed at this more than anything in the world. Besides, he's got his twenty-fifth reunion coming up soon back in Philadelphia..."

Grunts and nods of understanding went round the table.

"Bill's pretty tied up in knots about it. So would you pray for both of us, and especially my good brother, Bill?"

Everyone smiled and nodded, producing a magic moment at this table of guys. I was momentarily dumbfounded. I reached across the table and clenched Edmund's hand, giving it a man's squeeze. It's not a hug, but very close.

Tom closed by remembering every prayer request individually. I was quite touched by the whole meeting. I guess guys can open up to each other after all. And maybe, with their prayers, I could be ready for my reunion next month. Slimmer, smarter, and spiritually together.

Suddenly, I knew this was the right place for me to be. It didn't even matter all that much if I was a bit underdressed for the affair.

o sooner had I gotten into my car after the men's group when I heard a tapping on my car window. It was Edmund.

I rolled down the window manually, a feature all inexpensive cars have that the luxury models choose to ignore. Edmund smiled broadly, holding a copy of this morning's *Wall Street Journal* over his head as a makeshift umbrella in the very light drizzle.

"Whoa, Nellie! Are we off to a great start with this men's group or what?" he bellowed as if he were riding the range with a thousand little doggies.

"Yeah, this is pretty amazing, I must admit," I replied with a little reluctance. I've learned not to be too excited about a new group that forms, especially right at the start. The leadership usually translates that excitement into a dozen job assignments.

"This is a monumental day, my friend," Edmund added.

"What do you mean?" I asked, having grown weary many years ago of Edmund's version of Twenty Questions. When he knows something I don't know, he wears this silly little smirk on his face, making him look eight years old. I had a good morning, sure, but I still wasn't in any mood to dialogue with Alfalfa.

"Well, I was going to tell you before the breakfast this morning, but you were running a little late"—this is how guys communicate to one another the coded message, "You were late…that was bad…Tom was getting a little stressed…don't let it happen again!"—"so I didn't have time to tell you about my phone calls yesterday afternoon."

"Phone calls?"

"Yes. I've been a busy guy."

"Well, are you going to tell me about them or not?" I checked the clock on the dashboard of my car and it already said nine-fifteen. I couldn't be late again today. This wasn't a healthy pattern that I was beginning to fall into: Every time I was with Edmund, I became late for whatever was next.

In all fairness, I should clarify that it is *always* nine-fifteen on my clock, if one is basing his time system on the functions of the dashboard clock. Mine is in the identical condition of most dashboard clocks of the 1989 variety—broken.

Even with my mind wandering, I hadn't missed anything with Edmund. I guess that's one reason why I like him so much. He's not real hard to stay with, in the mental sense.

"So tell me, Edmund, what's going on?" I pressed him one last time.

"Okay, okay. Yesterday afternoon before I left the office I called around to some of the different health clubs in the area, and you'll be real proud of me, Bill. I saved us a lot of time. By comparing all the facilities, prices, and programs out there, I discovered the Pine Woods Health Club is the place for us. I spoke to a lady on the phone named Barbara Ann—"

"You mean like the Beach Boys' song?" I interrupted.

"That's right!" Edmund replied with rising energy. "Is that a good sign or what?"

Edmund and I are serious Beach Boys fans, and even though neither of us believe in omens, this was a wonderful twist of fate. Much of our life story is contained in those Beach Boys songs. Edmund listened to them as a teenager on the way to the beach in Southern California, and I listened on my annual trip to the shore at Atlantic City.

(Edmund and I have never quite figured out why Los Angeles kids go to the "beach," while Philadelphia kids go to the "shore." Frankly the only difference we've ever come up with is that in Southern California the ocean is on the left, and in Atlantic City, it is on the right.)

The Beach Boys' music was one of the first things that brought Edmund and me together. He was over at his parents' house, which is next to mine. I had the album *The Beach Boys Today* playing loudly from inside the house while I was raking pine needles outside.

Anyway, Edmund was so intrigued by the strains of *Help Me Rhonda* (the album version, not the single that got all the radio air time) coming from my house, he marched right over, introduced himself, and we began a fascinating journey with the Wilson brothers, their cousins, and their friends.

Edmund and I don't see eye-to-eye on all Beach Boys matters. He likes the car songs better than the surfer tunes, and I am the exact opposite. Of the non-Wilson members, he always liked Mike Love, whereas I gravitated toward Al Jardine.

But we share a lot of the same sentiments, also. We both can remember hoping and praying that the Beach Boys were Christians when they came out with the song "God Only Knows." Surely only a true believer would sing a song in praise of God's omnipotence.

We would both daydream about actually having the dilemma that makes up the lyrics for "California Girls." How we would love to imagine having hip girlfriends on the East Coast, Midwest farmer's daughters, Southern girls with the way they talk, and Northern girls with the way they kiss. How could we get them all to move to our town?

But unquestionably the favorite song for Edmund and me was "Barbara Ann." We both have happy recollections of purchasing the album *Beach Boys Party,* from which this single is lifted. Recorded live, in a room full of people, this album was classic before it was released.

Why do Edmund and I like *Barbara Ann* so much? What does that song have that is unlike any others? The answer is quite simple:

Mistakes.

Remember how they got all the girl's names confused in that latter verse? And the more they sang, the more jumbled it became—some of them just sang the same girl's name over and over.

This song speaks of humanity. Flawed man. Not bigger-than-life rock stars, but real, local garage-band vocalists who occasionally botch up the words. This is why the Beach Boys are special. This is why we will still pay large sums of money to see them wheeled out on stage to sing their songs, with or without their false teeth.

So when Edmund told me the lady at the health club was named Barbara Ann, you can understand why this was significant. It was like Mandy to a Barry Manilow fan, Lucille to a Kenny Rogers fan, or Michelle, Ma Belle, to a McCartney fan.

I focused once again on Edmund. He still stood outside my car, leaning toward my window, his *Wall Street Journal* now much damper. Edmund's a good man. He'll always wait for me to come back from my little distractions before continuing his conversation.

"So, anyway," he continued, "we have a noon appointment today with Barbara Ann over at the club."

I nodded in approval of Edmund's plan.

"She wants to show us around the facility, explain some of the equipment they use and get us more familiar with what Pine Woods Health Club has to offer."

"Thanks for doing all this stuff, Edmund."

"No problem. So I'll see you there, right?"

"Count on me."

We gave each other high fives (the male hug) and went our separate ways.

Work was as stressful as ever. Dr. Floyd mumbled his personal mantra, "The communications department, as we know it, may cease to exist at any moment," to anyone close enough to hear it. Unfortunately, it's hard to ignore the boss. If the senile old grouse in the company sweeps the floors, he's a cute character, but if he signs the checks, he's an acute inconvenience.

I had difficulty paying attention to my work. Not only had I come from a potentially life-changing meeting, I was just minutes away from a tour of a fitness center with Barbara Ann. In all the years of singing that song, it suddenly occurred to me that I had never actually met a woman named Barbara Ann.

My class ended at eleven-fifteen. Unlike the days of elementary school, when a student would hang back at the bell, shyly walk up to your desk and leave you an apple, college kids clear a classroom with the speed of nuclear energy. The bell rings at eleven-fifteen and I can always count on hearing the "click" made by the big classroom clock when it moves from eleven-fifteen to eleven-sixteen. And I hear it alone.

Gathering my loose papers, I packed everything in my well-worn, brown-leather satchel, turned out the lights, closed the door, and headed out the building across the quad's courtyard to my office. Seven pink slips indicating phone messages were taped on my door, and five large manila envelopes filled with interoffice mail blocked my entry.

Unlocking my door, I kicked the interoffice mail into my office. I peeled off the phone messages without ever looking to see who they were from. And naturally, I didn't pick up the phone to check my voice mail or return calls.

None of this clutter was essential right then. What matters was that I stop by the men's room to take one more stab at combing my hair, tucking in my shirttail, and washing my face. I needed to look good. I had a noon appointment with "You've got me rockin' and a rollin', rockin' and a reelin', Barbara Ann, Ba, Ba, Ba, Barbara Ann."

Granted, grown men aren't supposed to behave like this. For all I knew Barbara Ann was a married grandmother with thirteen kids and twenty-seven grandkids, three months away from retirement, into sack dresses that fit, and sported whiskers.

But hope springs eternal. It might not all be true. She might be single.

Driving out of the faculty parking lot, I leaned to the right and briskly punched the button on the glove compartment. If I wasn't mistaken, I had a small bottle of aftershave tucked away in the back somewhere. *Now might be a good time to break it out,* I thought, *the finishing touch for a charmer like me.*

As is so often the case, once the glove compartment door swung open, a thousand points of fright came spilling out of its depths, adding to the clutter already on the front passenger floor. The dumpster's waterfall included an array of objects that someone felt it necessary to save rather than discard:

—A McDonald's annex. We have enough napkins, ketchup, coffee stirrers, and sweet-and-sour sauce packets to feed the next Billy Graham crusade.

—Road maps. Considered by some an essential part of every glove box, I can agree in principle yet am confused as to why a Honda that never leaves Pine Woods, California, is the proud possessor of a map of New England.

—Cassette tapes and covers. Hundreds belched forth from my glove compartment, all of them warped from too much sun. Of course, none of the tapes corresponded to the boxes. So where were these tapes, since the boxes were empty? I sighed over the classic Christian cassette boxes. It's been too long since I listened to Evie Tornquist or B. J. Thomas.

—Emergency information. My car insurance information, vehicle registration, auto club card, and other important papers were meticulously wrapped around a red emergency flare. When a police officer pulled me over for speeding a few weeks back, he wanted to see my license, vehicle registration, and proof of insurance. But the latter two documents had kinda melted around the flare. Thankfully, the officer was apparently Christian. While I was rummaging for my stuff, I heard him mumble, "Wow, I haven't heard Evie Tornquist in years! I used to have the biggest crush on her!"

—Sunglasses. We have enough sunglasses in my glove compartment to spur a hostile takeover of Foster Grant. But only one pair is not broken, and the trick is to find that pair while doing sixty-five miles per hour down the freeway.

—Miscellaneous. I don't know anyone who actually places gloves in the glove compartment (though you wonder about a guy like Dr. Graydon). We had old socks, Popsicle sticks, tubes of glue, screwdrivers, K-mart sales slips from 1989, a roll of Lifesavers candy that would require a blowtorch to separate the "O's," a program from one of Brandon's football games, and my nineteen-year-old daughter Betsy's class picture—from eighth grade.

To my dismay, there was no aftershave. Unless one counts a melted tube of Chapstick, the glove compartment is void of toiletry items. By the time I jammed everything back into the box, while still attempting to drive, I found myself at the health club anyway, so I parked the car, right next to Edmund's Lexus. I checked myself in the rearview mirror one last time and hustled toward the front door.

Even before I opened the double-glass doors, I could see Edmund talking with the woman I assumed to be Barbara Ann. My body did a complete muscle spasm as I caught my first glimpse of her. Gorgeous...

a goddess. About five-feet-five, short blonde hair, big blue eyes, and a smile that could melt Greenland (or is it Iceland? No, my fifth-grader taught me that Iceland is green and Greenland is ice).

It took a millisecond to see that she believed in her product. All the body fat people like this lose must somehow be magically passed onto people like me at night while we sleep. Even more amazing about Barbara Ann was the ring finger on her left hand bore no token of matrimony. No whiskers, she wasn't fat, she was too young to be a grandmother and, best of all, she appeared to be *single*.

There was a God.

Once inside, I proceeded to engage in every middle-aged man's reflexive action upon spying a beautiful woman. I sucked in my gut the very best I could.

Edmund, already conversing with Barbara Ann, was somewhat red-faced from talking while holding in his gut at the same time. I made a mental note to let him do the talking, and I would just concentrate on looking fabulous, dahling.

"This must be Bill," Barbara Ann said as she turned and looked my direction.

Sheepishly, I nodded, words not yet able to come freely.

"I'm Barbara Ann, and I'll be your guide around Pine Woods Health Club this afternoon. I think you will really enjoy our facilities, and best of all, I want to tell you right from the start that we pride ourselves around here in *personalizing* every individual's exercise program. Part of my job is to see to it that you are benefiting from our club."

I was liking this better and better all the time. Edmund was too, but he was married, so it didn't count.

"Now, if you guys will follow me, I think we'll start with a brief tour of our building and grounds."

Edmund and I followed her around like a couple of puppy dogs, not even pausing at fireplugs.

"This first room is filled with equipment for our PACE class," she said, pointing to a room to our right. Once inside the room, she once again turned and faced us. "Do either of you know about PACE?"

At the moment she glanced at us we both shook our heads and sucked in our guts with the precise unison of a military drill.

"PACE is a thirty-minute class that is a circuit-training kind of experience. We work on cardiovascular training and resistance training. It's a full body workout and we have found it to be an efficient and effective workout for our members."

I was taken by her excellent word choices, use of gestures, and proper diction. She was giving an A-speech in my class. It never dawned on me that Barbara Ann was quoting a spiel that she had given a thousand times before.

"As you can see, we have machines that target the work on your chest, your shoulders, your arms, your stomach, your quads, your calves, your inner thighs, and your outer thighs."

At the mention of all these body parts, Edmund and I unconsciously rolled our shoulders back, stood taller, tightened our leg muscles, and made every attempt to look like bodybuilders.

"I might add that we provide an instructor who takes you through the PACE class," she continued. "That way, he or she can time you, motivate you, and hold you accountable for participating in every station of the circuit. We also play music in the background to help you take your mind off your workout."

"What kind of music do you play?" I burst out, experiencing firsthand the trauma of trying to speak and inhale simultaneously. I actually became a little lightheaded.

"Good question, Bill," she smiled back and I thought I would float away.

"We play all kinds of music. We play country-western, 1940s Big Bands, rock and roll, reggae, oldies, you name it…"

"Do you play Beach Boys?" Edmund blurted out, reading my mind.

"Sure. Sometimes. We do it all."

Barbara Ann was now guiding us out of the PACE room into the next room down the long, well-lit, fully mirrored hall. *People sure do like to look at themselves in places like this,* I thought, never daring to make such an obscene comment to my tour guide. By not looking at myself in any of the mirrors, I could continue my mental illusion that I looked like Robert Redford.

"This is the room that holds all our cardiovascular equipment. As you can see, we have Stairmasters, treadmills, and upright and semirecumbent bikes as well."

A semirecumbent bike must be half-bicycle, half-cucumber, I reasoned. But neither Edmund nor I were brave enough to ask for clarification.

"Out this door, you'll notice we have four tennis courts," Barbara Ann continued. "They're clay courts, very well kept, as you can see. We have them well lit for early morning and nighttime play as well. Do either of you play tennis?" Barbara Ann once again turned to look at us.

Edmund and I hadn't played tennis in at least ten years.

"I do," I politely lied.

"So do I," Edmund joined in.

"Well, you guys will love these courts. They're great. Behind the tennis court is a full-sand volleyball court. I know we're pretty far away from the beach, but we try to give a little flavor of it by providing that court. It's quite popular, especially with our younger members."

"I'll make a note of that," I spoke without even thinking, desperately trying to impress her.

Stupidity on autopilot, that's me.

By now we were back inside, coming toward the front of the building again, but moving down a different corridor. "Here's the favorite spot in the whole club," Barbara Ann winked as she smiled. "It's the Nutrition Bar. We sell all kinds of healthy food and drinks here."

The thought of food caused Edmund and me to brighten up. I was giving up my lunch for this tour, so I was particularly interested in what might be available.

"The favorite item here is a Smoothee. It's a fruit-juice drink that's loaded with extras like protein powder. It's dynamite."

The thought of protein powder led to a mental picture of gathering up all the chalk dust in one of my classrooms and placing it in a blender along with a banana and some orange juice. It left me with a strong feeling of *bland*.

"As you can see, the Nutrition Bar is right next to the door that leads to our indoor pool. It's seventy-five feet long and four feet deep. We keep it precisely at eighty-three degrees, so it's quite comfortable."

"Why eighty-three degrees?" Edmund asked, as I snorted to indicate my that's-a-stupid-question sentiment.

"That's a very thoughtful question," Barbara Ann responded to Edmund. Her tone left me feeling betrayed. "It's actually kind of a funny story around here at the club." At this point she leaned in as if she were going to tell us a secret.

"The truth is," she whispered in a loud stage whisper (which was really no softer than her regular speaking voice), "we have a lot of senior citizens who like to swim here. They are always asking us to heat the pool to eighty-six degrees. But the rest of the club members want it at a cooler temperature, like eighty. So, do you get what we've done?"

"You've split the difference!" Edmund immediately answered before I had the chance.

"That's right!" Barbara Ann was glowing now.

"I know," Edmund added. "I'm an accountant."

"Oooohhh," Barbara Ann gushed, sensing a sale was imminent. "I'm impressed."

I sucked my gut in even further, realizing I couldn't compete with the exciting world of being a CPA. I was reduced to raw animal magnetism.

"Now we'll need to split up at this point," Barbara Ann continued. "I want you guys to walk through the men's locker room. While you're in there you will see we have a hot tub and a sauna, which are always available. Go ahead and take your time. I'll go through the women's locker room and meet you on the other side. Just come through the door."

Edmund and I slowly observed the locker facilities. There wasn't really anything out of the ordinary that caused us to walk so slowly, but the truth was we both needed a break from holding in our guts. My abdominal muscles had been screaming ever since we passed the tennis courts, and exhaling never felt so exhilarating.

Barbara Ann was waiting for us on the other side. "As we walk back to my office, don't forget to notice we also have four racquetball courts, including this front court that is clear Plexiglas on all four walls with room for a total of sixty-five spectators on each of the four sides."

The thought of playing racquetball in front of sixty-five people struck further pain in my abdomen.

Her next question caught both of us guys off guard. "Is either of you married?"

"HE IS!" I veritably screamed, pointing an accusing finger at poor Edmund.

"Do you have kids?" she followed up.

"Yes," he whispered, but bellowed, "SO DOES HE!" now pointing the finger of doom my direction.

"Okay," Barbara Ann replied, rolling her eyes ever so slightly to indicate she wasn't quite sure what that was all about. "I just thought I'd ask, because both of you will be glad to know we have family packages and we also have a fully staffed, beautifully decorated child-care center right here on the premises."

Edmund and I made a quick attempt at regrouping as we sat down in her office to discuss the one last issue…money.

"How much is all this gonna cost?" Edmund asked as we looked at the pictures of Barbara Ann with famous physically fit people that decorated her office walls.

"I think you'll find that we are very competitive," she began. A flipchart of options became the focal point as she placed it on her desk blotter facing us. "We have per-month plans, we have semiannual plans, and we have annual plans," she continued.

The budget choice was clearly between food money or fit money. Did we want to eat, or exercise?

"The per month plan will include an additional one-time-only fifty-dollar application fee. If you sign up for the semiannual plan, we reduce that to twenty-five dollars, and if you're smart, you'll go for the annual plan that waives the application fee entirely. You have to admit, it's a good deal."

This brought vague recollections of the used car salesman reminding me how good a deal I was getting on the used car that broke down the next week through the abuse of sitting in my garage. But I'd never done business with a used car salesman who looked anything like Barbara Ann.

"Could you give us a few minutes to talk about this privately?" Edmund asked Barbara Ann. She smiled, nodded, said she completely understood, stood up, grabbed a legal pad, and walked out of the office, closing the door behind her.

"What do you think?" Edmund asked me.

"I don't know. What do you think?"

"Well, it's kinda more money than I thought it would be, but it really is something we need to do to get ourselves in shape." Edmund was getting to the place where he was rational in his thinking again. Marriage will do that for you, yet I was still a little out there.

"Should we go for it?" I asked him.

His next statement threw me. "Do you think this is the right thing to do?"

The right thing? I was having so much fun living this dream world, I hadn't even thought about what was right. But we really did need the workouts, right?

"The words of an old hymn are coming to mind," I answered Edmund as a smile appeared on my face.

"What hymn?" he asked.

"I went to a dance—" I hummed the tune for him.

"Looking for romance?" he asked.

I nodded smugly.

Edmund was smiling now, too.

"Let's take a chance, Edmund. We need this. I say we go for it."

So that's how Edmund and I came to sign up for a year's membership at the Pine Woods Health Club. Sure, it was expensive, but our health was worth it.

It's probably important to make two final observations in order to put this story in complete perspective:

1) Neither Edmund nor I ever saw Barbara Ann again, though we looked for her diligently during our next three workouts.

2) After three visits, we gave up, and we haven't returned since.

11

For the next couple of days I couldn't get one thought out of my mind. Tom had suggested we recommend book titles from our own daily reading and Quiet Time. The idea nagged at me, gnawed at me, haunted me deep down in my soul. I genuinely desired a consistent early morning time alone with God. But it seemed to rarely take place.

I have been convicted about my lack in this area on numerous occasions. From the time I was a child, the key to getting my attention has remained—*guilt.*

All the minister needed to do is was talk about taking time each day for God to speak to us through his Word and for us to speak to him through prayer. Instantly I was filled with remorse, vowing that this time it would be different: I would communicate with the most holy God in heaven.

On the positive side, if I could somehow add up all the Mondays that I read the Bible and prayed, I think I could probably come up with *years* of devoted Quiet Times with the Lord.

Plus, if you add all the New Year's resolutions to read the Bible through in a year, I have another thirty to sixty days where I faithfully plodded through the first few chapters of Genesis. (Of course, now with the advent of *The One Year Bible*, that would be two days of Genesis, Matthew, Psalms, and Proverbs, so I continue to make even more progress thanks to the miracle of Christian publishing.)

Of course, this being the twentieth century, the Bible alone isn't really enough. We now have access to devotional guides that direct us through the uncharted waters of Scripture. (If anyone needs help in understanding the idiosyncrasies of Isaiah or the theology of the Thessalonians, it's me).

So, bright and early the next morning, I was out of bed, seated at my desk, Bible opened, devotional guides spread all over the desktop, prayer journal in hand, commentaries, theological dictionaries, a concordance and Bible atlas at my side, ready for any issue that would rear its ugly head in an attempt to thwart my personal time of communion with the Lord.

I had all the tools for The Perfect Quiet Time. Opening my copy of the Scriptures to its center, I decided that the book of Psalms was always a wonderful place to start.

Shout joyfully to the Lord, all the earth.
Serve the Lord with gladness;
Come before him with singing.
You have now read as much as your mind will hold;
It is time for your mind to drift off.
Think, my child, think of grocery lists and chores.
Come before my presence with distractions.
For that leaky faucet will not fix itself, will it?
Know ye, that I am here when your mind refocuses.
Perhaps tomorrow.
To everything there is a season.
Go, Dodgers!

You purists will search in vain for this passage of Scripture. But, regrettably, this is how my private reading of the Bible tends to look. The road to hell is paved with good distractions.

As a young boy I remember waking up each morning and attempting to read my Bible and its partner, *Our Daily Bread.* Baked by the DeHaan family, this booklet arrived monthly. The daily regimen was clear: read the assigned passage of Scripture, then read the little devotional story that took up most of the page. After each story came the daily challenge. In one pithy sentence, the DeHaans summarized everything a Christian needed to know to live a happy, productive, godly life in the next twenty-four hours—before needing the next slice of bread.

Believe me, it was quite tempting to go straight to the bottom line on occasion, overlooking the story of how Aunt Nanette's quilt reminded her of Balaam's donkey. Some days you just wanted to read: "Don't be bored, serve the Lord!" Or some other curious maxim.

As I grew older I went through a phase where I believed I was not getting much out of *Our Daily Bread* because it was being sent to me free. They always included a donation envelope, but I never sent in one. Clearly I was misguided as a youth, choosing to spend my money on baseball cards, model airplanes, and Hershey Bars, rather than supporting the DeHaan and Son Bakery.

I can also recall the stage I refer to as the When I Became a Man, I Put Away Childish Things Stage. This was one of the more recent phases for me. I spurned the *Breads* and the *Walks,* choosing the type of devotional literature that has stood the test of time.

I refer, of course, to *The Classics.* A friend whom I respect greatly told me that he had his daily devotions in Oswald Chambers' book, *My Utmost for His Highest.* It sounded very mature, adult, and spiritual to me, so I decided to purchase a copy.

Upon entering the Christian bookstore, I hit the mother lode. This title was available in dozens of different styles and sizes. There were also quite a few that provided forewords by people like Oswald's relatives, noted theologians, statesmen, and sports figures. (The volume with the Mike Singletary endorsement was very tempting.)

These editions come with covers in a variety of colors. My eye caught a hot-pink leather version that was quite conspicuous sitting there next to the more quiet pastel colors. I assumed that the hot pink must be for that person who has everything when it comes to devotional literature. Certainly few of us can brag of a hot-pink Chambers.

No price was too great, so I purchased the cheap paperback version and began my relationship with Oswald. It was harder than I expected. I learned what makes something a classic. It's timeless—meaning no reference to Walkmans, ball games, picnics, or television shows. It's just be holy, man, be holy!

For a guy like me, Chambers is good, but not before 10:00 A.M. and not after 5:00 P.M.

Most recently I have gone through my "journaling" phase. This is quite popular these days, men encouraging other men to get in touch with their feelings, emotions, and most private spiritual thoughts. The idea is that by staring at the blank page, you will hear God speak to you. He will tell you what to write down. Stop that doodling in the margins, for the Lord himself will speak!

But I have a bad case of The Wandering Mind. I want to write good thoughts to God and I want to listen as He responds with great thoughts back. But my journal entries border on a seventh-grader's secret diary, complete with the little lock and key.

Today I am struggling with the concept of heartburn. I fear the very real dilemma that I may need to give up pepperoni on my pizza. Thinking of this causes me to cry out, saying, "Why Lord? Why?" I feel ashamed, for I have been faithfully taking medication to offset this spiritual disease, only to find out it has been ineffective in my case. I have jars of Tums and Rolaids around the house, but I have been mistakenly taking Certs for the last three days and they have done nothing for my heartburn (although I must say my breath is minty fresh).

Lord, speak to me concerning my future with one of your good and perfect gifts...pepperoni. Help me to know your will and then act on it.

This does not seem to be the sort of spiritual warfare that Tom had in mind. But I tend to think, if God is the God of the mountains, the God of the blue skies, and the God of the oceans, is he not also the God of the pepperoni?

Another constant dilemma I have in journaling is the inability to do it consistently. Before each entry, I jot down the day and the date. Looking back over my last journal, page one reads:

SATURDAY, JANUARY 1, 1994

The heading on the next entry is fairly self-explanatory:

FRIDAY, AUGUST 25, 1995

My eyes darted open. I'd fallen asleep at my desk and drooled all over my open Bible, more precisely all over the one-hundredth Psalm. I like this psalm. I even had it underlined in red ink in my Bible. Now the drool has mixed with the ink, so it appears to read: "Shoot joyfully fo the Lorp, all tha earck."

This wasn't an encouraging start on my quest to get it together spiritually. "Kenny Kramer doesn't doze off one verse into his Bible reading,"

I scolded myself. "The key is discipline. Stay focused, hang tough, keep cool.

"I need to shift gears," I decided. "I'll pray, and perhaps I'll return to reading a little later." As I prepared to pray, I placed a list of requests in front of me that I wanted to remember. But, alas, this was no help.

Dear Lord:

Thank you for this day. Thank you for all your wonderful gifts (I need to stop by Sierra Sports to see if they have that Syracuse basketball jersey for Brandon) that you have given to me and my family. (Does Ben need a ride home from school today, or is that tomorrow?) This is a beautiful day that you have made. (If it's so nice, I should do something productive like go out jogging or something, but jogging is so painful!)

Help me to focus on you today, dear Lord. (Perhaps the reason I keep having these headaches is the fact that I need to have my eyes examined.) I have a few requests to bring before you, Lord. (Don't forget to pay bills.) Please help Edmund get it together. (I'd have a much better chance to get it together if I drove around in a Lexus like Edmund does!) Help my sweet daughter Betsy to do well while she is away in college. (I need to write her a letter.) Keep BJ safe today. (Check the brakes on his Honda.) Help Brandon to start at his position on the football team. (Grab the sports section of the newspaper before going to work.) Give Ben what he needs to do well in his social studies class. (Oops: I think Ben already took his big test and I forgot to ask how he did. Make sure to do that today!) Keep Bo from getting a cold, dear God. He has the sniffles. (I need to call about the results of my blood test.) Please help me get my life together, so I can wow everyone at my high-school reunion. (I need major assistance here, Lord.) Help me to do well at work. (I've still got to trim my budget! Yikes! It's due today!)

Uhh, Lord, I'm going to have to cut this short. I just remembered some work I didn't do. I know how important it is to be a good testimony at work. (You're doomed, buddy. Dr. Floyd is gonna eat you for lunch!)

I love you, Lord. Amen.

Before leaving my desk, I wrote myself a little note in my journal under the date:

I need to make an appointment to speak with the pastor. I am becoming firmly convinced that I am suffering from Spiritual Attention Deficit Disorder. It really is SADD.

I had just finished with my Friday afternoon Public Speaking 101 class.

And Charlotte Spencer had just ended her three-to five-minute persuasive speech on why everyone should sell Amway products.

I always feel in a bind when students present these sorts of speeches. Obviously Charlotte had swiped her material from pros at motivational, pump 'em up meetings. It doesn't seem quite fair to pit Charlotte against, say, Samuel Martinez, a recent arrival from Mexico, who earlier—as far as I can tell—tried to argue the medicinal uses of the persimmon.

After class, one student stayed after the bell. His name is Charlie Bradley, and he has that California surf look going, though it is winter-ized by a plaid flannel shirt. An earring in his left earlobe is just visible beneath his blond hair, and he's got a half-exposed tattoo on his right forearm. A backpack slung over his shoulder completed the look.

I knew why Charlie was loitering. He was scheduled to give his per-suasive speech on Monday, and he was not ready. So, he would give a longer, more involved persuasive speech after class today in an effort to convince me that he needed more time. He approached me with his hands in his pockets, shoulders slouched, and a look on his face that suggested irregularity over a three-week period.

"Mr. Butterworth, can I talk to you for a second?"

"Sure, Charlie, what can I do for you?" I did a good job of pretending I didn't know.

"Well, you probably don't realize this, but I am scheduled to give my persuasive speech in class on Monday."

"Well, what do you know!" I exclaimed. I try to give the student the benefit of the doubt as long as I can.

"Yeah, it's on Monday, for sure," Charlie responded, pulling a hand out of his pocket to brush back a wave of blond hair that had fallen in front of his eyes. "I'm, like, really swamped with work from my other classes this semester, and so I guess what I'm asking is, could I possibly, you know, have a little extension of, say, a couple a weeks, before I have to give my presentation?"

I allowed the silence to eat away at his belly while I contemplated what he asked. I tried to be gracious, but the request for "a couple of weeks" signaled to me that Charlie had "swimmer's ear" in both ears.

"Tell me about the work you have for your other classes," I offered.

"Well..." Charlie stuttered, "I have this mega-report on the political outcomes of the Civil War for my American History class. I don't even know who we were fighting against and the paper's gotta be, like, twenty pages typed, man. And they won't let you double-space, you gotta single-space!"

"When is that paper due?" I calmly asked.

His head dropped, and I knew I had scored. "Next month," he mumbled.

"Uh-huh." I replied matter-of-factly. "What other work do you have that is due in the more immediate future?"

His body language told me that victory was mine.

"That's the only other class I'm taking," Charlie confessed, sensing that a bummer of a breaker was about to crest over his head.

"I see," I said. And Charlie knew he'd gone under.

"Have you done much in the way of preparation for your persuasive speech yet, Charlie?"

"A little."

"How much is 'a little'?"

"None."

"Then it sounds to me like you have a pretty busy weekend ahead of you."

"No chance of a delay?"

"No chance."

"Thanks a lot, Mr. Butterworth," Charlie replied, sarcasm dripping out of his mouth.

I attempted to give my time-proven lecture on life management. But Charlie had already spun around on his steel-toed work boots and proceeded to storm out of the room in protest of "this totally lame professor" as he would later describe the situation to his friends at the student lounge.

Gathering my papers, I walked back to my office, wondering what the future will hold for students like Charlie, and Charlotte, and Samuel. My guess was that Charlie would struggle for a few more years in life, and that Samuel would be a real go-getter.

But eventually they'd both be working for Charlotte.

Back at my office, I was once again greeted by the festive pink slips of paper that decorated my door like Mardi Gras. I perused them quickly. No emergencies, and no messages from my kids. But my eye was taken by the ASAP signal on a message from Edmund.

I wish it were tax season so this guy had something to do! I thought. But deep down, I knew that Edmund was a Godsend.

After speed-dialing only to stumble through a maze of receptionists, personal assistants, middle managers, and partners who eventually connected me with the person to whom I wished to speak, I greeted Edmund gratefully.

"Bill, I'm so glad it's you! Thanks for calling right back. I've got great news!" Edmund was almost breathless.

"What is it?"

"Kenny Kramer is still in the area! Can you believe it?"

"Where?"

"At the Sacramento Community Center. He's giving a lecture as part of their *Meeting Community Needs* series. It's really a great opportunity to hear him again. And get this, if I'm not mistaken, he is speaking on the topic *Helping Your Children Get It Together.* Isn't that cool?"

"Um. Ahhh...Hmm," I enthused. Part of me felt grateful to the guy who convicted me about getting my life together, but another part of me resented how hard it was to accomplish.

I had been trying *so hard* over the last week to get my life together. I made a mental list:

—I got a *complete* physical.

—I plugged into a men's group.

—I tried to pay closer attention to my work.

—I attempted to be a better dad.

—I reacquainted myself with Quiet Time.

—I joined a health club.

—I started to sort my screws out in the garage.

—I bought some low-fat toothpaste.

—I planned to toss any items in the fridge that I couldn't recognize—soon.

—I *almost* locked Bo in his messy room until he'd cleaned it up.

—I *tried* not to lie too much on my response form for the reunion.

—I *thought* about volunteering at the soup kitchen...

"Anyway," Edmund pushed on, "guess when he's gonna give the lecture?"

"When?"

"Tonight!"

"Tonight?"

"That's right. And I've already got tickets for you and all your boys."

"My boys? Tickets for my boys?" Now I was *really* in shock. My boys and lectures went together like Jerry Falwell and the musician formerly known as Prince.

"Correct. Actually, I got them for us, but when I called home Jenny informed me that one of the kids has some kind of recital tonight, so there's no way we can go."

"No way?"

"No way."

"I see."

"So the five tickets are yours, my friend. My treat."

This is how men end up attending lectures with their sons.

I glanced down at my watch and realized most of the boys would be home from school by now, so I dialed our number.

"He-ell-oo?" Brandon whined. The other boys always sounded pleasant, but Brandon had this pain thing going.

"Brandon, it's Dad."

"Hey, Dad. What's for dinner?"

"Nice to hear your voice, too, my son. Listen, we're all going out tonight."

"For dinner?"

"No."

"To a movie?"

"No."

"A concert?"

"Close."

"Close?"

"Yeah."

"Whaddya mean 'close,' Dad?"

"Well, it's like a soloist, except he's not singing."

"If he's not singing, what is he doing?"

"Speaking."

"Speaking?"

"Yes, Brandon, tonight we're all attending a lecture."

The silence on the other end of the phone was more frightening than anything he could have said.

"Brandon?"

More silence.

"Brandon, are you there?"

The silence was finally broken by a new voice.

"Hello?"

"Ben?"

"Oh, hi Dad!" Ben answered. "What did you say to Brandon? He ran out of the room—"

"Ben, listen to me. We're going out to a lecture tonight."

"Why, Daddy?" he interrupted. "Have we been neglecting our chores?"

"No, Ben, this is not a punishment, it is something I thought you would all appreciate. I have heard this man speak before and he is really entertaining. I think you'll enjoy it and benefit from it, if you just give it a chance."

"Okay," Ben droned.

"That's my boy," I replied. "Tell the other boys to dress up in coats and ties. I'll be home in an hour, and then we'll scoot."

"Dad, I don't have a coat that fits anymore," Ben said, a slight hint of hope in his voice. Perhaps no jacket meant no lecture.

"Back in my closet are some of my old blue blazers. Try one of them on and hopefully one will fit you."

"You usually don't want me wearing your clothes, Dad."

"Well, tonight it's just fine," I answered. "Don't forget to tell the other boys, okay? Gotta run so I can get home. I love you, Ben. Bye-bye."

Hanging up the phone, I tried to imagine the reaction going on at the house. Wailing? Bad language? Fire-setting? Would some of them run away?

The clearer the possibilities became, the more I tried to block them from my mind.

This was going to be quite a night.

By the time I arrived home, the good news was that everyone was dressed, ready to go. The bad news was that everyone had virtually wiped out my clothes closet, leaving me little or no choice of wardrobe. Ben was wearing an old blazer of mine with tarnished gold buttons and lapels as wide as barn doors.

BJ wore my double-breasted blue blazer, my most current of blazers. I was just about to protest when Brandon walked in with still another of my sport coats (a gray tweed number) on his body. I sighed when Bo came down the hall. He was wearing a jacket of his own, and I silently thanked God I didn't have a jacket small enough for a ten-year-old to wear.

Then I noticed other signs of looting. BJ and Brandon were both wearing my dress shirts. Ben and Bo were wearing my neckties. And my good overcoat was draped over BJ's arm.

"Don't we look great, Pops?" BJ beamed widely, choosing to take the offensive.

"You all have excellent taste in clothes," I mumbled weakly. Hustling to my once-full closet, I dug out a gray suit that had survived the rumble.

Before anyone could argue, we were all buckled in the Honda, heading down Interstate 80 on our way for our seven-thirty appointment at the Sacramento Community Center.

"What's this all about?" BJ asked, assuming his usual role as the boys' spokesman.

"We're going to hear the speaker that I heard at the Men's Retreat," I explained.

"Kenny Kramer?" Bo piped up. Bo was amazing with names, a trait he did not inherit from his father.

"That's right, Bo, Kenny Kramer."

"Why do we have to go, Dad?" Ben asked through great pain.

"Well, as you know, I was really moved by some of the stuff this guy had to say. Part of his presentation was on the importance of growing intellectually and emotionally, so I thought this would be an excellent opportunity for all of us to do that. Plus, Edmund says he is speaking about kids."

"Yeah, attending a lecture sure sounds intellectual," BJ added, eyes rolling.

"Does 'intellectual' mean 'boring'?" Bo whispered to Brandon.

"No," he grunted. "'Intellectual' means big-time boring—boring beyond belief—call 911 boring. This could very easily kill you."

Bo swallowed hard, and I saw his eyes widen as I watched him through my rearview mirror. "He's just fooling with you, Bo," I comforted. "You'll like it, don't worry."

Noticing that I was watching him in the mirror, Bo did his best to put a smile on his face. It was a brave effort, but the result was as flimsy as the smile he produces when he gets underwear for Christmas.

We parked close to the Center and walked into the lobby. It was a proud moment for me, striding into a lecture with four very handsome young men, all dressed in coats and ties. They hadn't been dressed like this since Aunt Harriet died two years ago. (We go to one of those churches that encourages everyone to dress *casual*. After all, we do live in California.) Hair combed, shoes semishined, faces clean. It was magic.

I wished I had brought the camera, but of course, it was still at home loaded with twenty exposures taken at Christmas, the last sixteen shots to be used at Easter.

We got our programs from an usher. "This will be good to draw pictures on," Ben counseled Bo as they were each handed one. Bo nodded as Brandon asked the usher, "May I please have an extra one for my sister who is in the ladies' room?" The other boys smirked.

Naturally, they were well supplied with pencils, pens, markers, and highlighters.

Imagine the shock to my system when I read the program and in doing so discovered that Edmund was wrong. Dead wrong. Kenny Kramer was not speaking on *Helping Your Children Get It Together.* The topic in the program was simply listed as *Wholeness.*

Wholeness? I thought. *The boys are gonna shoot me full of wholeness by the time this session is over.* It was at that point a strange smell came over the Community Center. It's a difficult odor to describe, but we've all smelled it.

It's the smell of boredom.

Forgetting the lecture series' decorum, the younger two boys bounced up and down on their theater seats as if they were minitrampolines. Before too long an elderly lady in a flowered dress marched boldly to the podium to introduce the speaker.

"Ladies and gentlemen, welcome to the sixth in a series of twelve lectures on *Meeting Community Needs* here at the Sacramento Community Center." Her voice was loud enough, but it had that old person's waver to it that caught my sons' attention, among other things.

"Look at all the jewelry she's wearing!" Ben observed. "She must be rich!"

"Look at all the wrinkles on her," Bo added with his characteristic bluntness. "She must be a hundred!"

"I'll bet you she was cute in her day," BJ winked. "I wonder if she has any single great-great-great-great-granddaughters."

The introduction for Kenny was completely lost on the boys as they took turns perfecting the stage whisper with each other. Fortunately, thunderous applause drowned them out as Kenny Kramer stepped to the lectern.

Of course, Kenny was dressed impeccably. At the retreat he was the picture of "Dressy/Casual," but tonight he was going for "Executive Do-rite." He wore a blue suit that was tailored to the nearest millimeter. His white shirt accented his deep tan, and, of course, the shirt was starched to the point that one could ski off it. His tie was red, gold, and navy blue horizontal stripes, knotted to perfection in the Windsor style. His hair was stylistically marbled to his head, as if it never moved, wavered, or grew an inch. The notes for his lecture were bound in a leather folder, in precisely the same navy blue color of his suit. If one looked closely, the words *Kenny Kramer* were embossed in gold on the lower right corner of the folio.

Kenny was one classy guy.

I nervously attempted to button my jacket, immediately intimidated by Kenny's appearance. Of course, buttoning my suit jacket was impossible, since I bought this suit about two thousand Tastykakes ago. *I've got to take up jogging,* I thought while applauding zero-body-fat Kenny.

As he began his remarks, I quickly ascertained that I was going to be hearing the same speech I had heard at the retreat. *This is why people become professional guest speakers,* I concluded. *They only have four or five speeches, so they just keep changing audiences and the title of the speeches. It's nice work if you can get it.*

The boys were in typical form for young men attending a lecture. There were many acute attacks of cotton mouth, requiring regular trips back to the lobby water fountain. This inevitably led to the junkets to the men's room. Seeing an old man excuse himself with a coughing attack, my boys were all simultaneously struck with a whooping hack that demanded immediate attention—back in the lobby.

There was a moment, albeit a split second in time, but nonetheless, a moment where all four boys were in their seats at the same time. I glanced down the row to see how they were reacting to all this. Bo was drawing a picture of a monster. Ben and Brandon were halfway through their seventh game of Hangman. To my amazement, BJ was actually listening! He laughed at the humorous moments, nodded occasionally, and even jotted down a thought or two on his program.

. I took what I could get. One out of four paying attention was only batting .250, but hey, this is paying attention at a lecture, not the Giants vs. A's World Series! All was not lost. BJ was getting it together mentally!

The lecture ended and I bought each of my sons a genuine souvenir Kenny Kramer T-shirt as a remembrance of their night of culture. In an effort to make Dad feel good, they put on their T-shirts—once they were safely in the car. Of course, they were all turned inside-out, but it was the thought that counted.

Driving home, I daydreamed a little. I remembered the old joke about the farmer who wanted his donkey to run in the Kentucky Derby. When asked why, the farmer replied, "Well, I know he wouldn't win, but I really thought the association would do him good!" ·

I tried to hang on to this idea later when I discovered that even BJ wasn't paying attention to the lecture. Suddenly I saw BJ growing up to be Charlie Spencer, surfer dude, professional non-public speaker. What I had mistaken for paying attention was really a boy getting into the music that played through tiny earphones attached to his Walkman.

13

I guess it was selective hearing. You know, one of those situations where you only hear certain parts of a conversation while unconsciously blocking out other parts. If you're married, I know you understand. Anyway, as I look back, all I can remember was:

"Hi, Bill, it's Tom Graham."

"Hey, Tom, it's nice of you to call me. What's up?"

"I was wondering if you'd like to join me for a little—"

"Join you?" (I love spending time with Tom. After all, he's sorta my hero.)

"And after we finish that we'll drive over to Starbucks and have a latte—"

"That sounds wonderful, buddy!"

"Yeah, it'll be a good chance to visit a bit—"

"Great! I'd like that." (Maybe he can give me some personal help on how to get things right!)

"I asked Edmund to join—"

"Sounds good, Tom."

"By the way, don't forget to wear loose-fitting clothes, if you haven't been...in a while."

"Okay," I said.

"All right, my friend, I'll see you Saturday at 10:00 A.M. at the entrance to Pioneer Park."

"I wouldn't miss it." (Why Pioneer Park?)

"I'll call you if it's raining too hard…. But we're tough, we can handle it, can't we?"

"You bet!" Rain never kept me from a Saturday morning Starbucks latte, I can assure you.

That was Tuesday. The phone rang at eight-thirty Saturday morning. Since my boys like to sleep in, phone calls on nonschool days automatically go to Dad.

"Hello?" I said a bit groggily into the receiver.

"Bill! It's Edmund!"

"Edmund? What time is it?"

"It's about eight-thirty, Mr. Sunshine. Tell me, how was the lecture last night?"

"Fine." (I sounded like one of my kids early in the morning. Brief, unhelpful, slurred.)

"Did Kenny Kramer knock it out of the ball park? I'll bet it was fabulous!"

"A home run, Edmund." I hoped this answer would quickly get him off the phone so I could get back to sleep.

"Did your boys absolutely love him?" Edmund persisted. Clearly, I was out of luck.

"I wouldn't say they *loved* him, but there were no ugly scenes of public disruption. I take that as a positive sign." I said this as diplomatically as possible. After all, Edmund *did* buy the tickets.

"Well that sounds good. So, you're ready for our morning jog with Tom?"

"Jog?" I was truly incredulous.

"Yeah. Tom said he called you earlier in the week and that you sounded excited about the prospect of us all getting together. Bill, it should be a riot!"

"Yikes! Edmund, I thought he was inviting us to Starbucks for a latte. I don't remember hearing anything about jogging. You know I'm not what you would call a real *jogger.*"

"Whoa, Nellie!" Edmund yelled. "You missed the biggest part of the conversation. Didn't he say anything about meeting him at the front of Pioneer Park at 10:00 A.M.?"

"Well...I guess I remember hearing something like that," I confessed.

"And he said he would call us if it was raining too hard. Does that ring a bell?"

"Yes, now that I do remember." With a sudden burst of enthusiasm, I glanced out my bedroom window to see if God was smiling down on us. He was. It was pouring rain. This was my out—it was raining too hard to go jogging.

"Well, Tom just called me," Edmund continued. "He wanted me to call you. He said if it's all right with us, he wants to keep our appointment. He thinks the rain will let up a couple of miles into our jog. So we're still on, buddy!"

Still in bed, I allowed the severity of that last statement to roll over me. *We are going jogging in the pouring rain, but the rain should let up several miles into our run.* I quietly assumed the fetal position.

"Let me remind you," Edmund continued, "this is your last shot at getting in shape before the reunion."

I sighed. "You're right, Edmund."

"The health club didn't happen, and to be honest, buddy, you don't look much different than you did before the weekend retreat. How will you impress anyone you knew twenty-five years ago? You've got to go on this run."

"Oh man," I said, "When you put it that way...."

"Jenny gave me this get-in-shape program from a magazine she was reading and it says if you run every day, eat only the bare essentials, and sleep completely wound in plastic wrap, you could lose five to seven pounds in less than a week."

"Wow," I said. "Would aluminum foil do the same thing? How about we forget the jog, and I'll sleep in anything you want?"

"No dice. It's final. I'll swing by at nine forty-five and pick you up. Okay, Bill?

"Bill?

"BILL?"

I was in a real bind. I needed to think this through. If I were going only with Edmund, I could cancel in a second, since I have no self-respect with Edmund. That's why he's my best friend. And perhaps if it were only Tom, I could come up with an excuse that would sound legit. All those years of hearing my students make excuses for speeches should have helped somehow. But, alas, I was stuck. Edmund knew every single excuse I have ever used in the last decade. He was too committed to my new life to allow this opportunity to pass by. No, it was time to wake up and smell the running shoes. I was going jogging and there was no way out short of death itself.

I said good-bye to Edmund and stumbled into the shower. "Fill me with power, you hot-watered shower!" I wailed. It was a little mantra I learned back in college.

I firmly hold to the philosophy that there is no life BSBC (before shower, before coffee). After the shower did its part, I toweled off and shuffled to the kitchen in my ugly green bathrobe to begin the coffee-maker's portion of human life-saving.

Back in the bedroom, I threw on faded sportswear from my previous careers with the New York Knicks and UCLA, and topped it with a T-shirt from Mr. Rogers' Neighborhood. It didn't match, but I didn't care. Finally, I found a pair of partially decomposed tennis shoes. It was either them or penny loafers. This took a minute, but I decided I didn't want to wear the penny loafers in the rain.

The sound of a Lexus horn outside my window startled me at precisely nine forty-five. I hadn't even had time to say good-bye to my children. Of course, they were all still asleep. Friday night was their one night to catch hours of late-night TV, calling it quits once the infomercials kicked in. Instinctively I reached for my wallet and keys, threw them into my sweatpants pockets, grabbed an old Dodger cap, and trotted out to meet Edmund.

"Looking good, buddy!" Edmund greeted me way too sincerely. Edmund was sporting a brand-new running suit in a pastel green. His hat, shoes, and socks were all marked with a "swoosh." Edmund is The Human Swoosh. And somewhere Nike is swooshing all the way to the bank.

"I should probably warn you," Edmund exhorted as I settled into his rich leather interior, "Tom is a pretty good runner, so it's gonna be real important that you and I establish our own pace."

"What are you saying, Edmund?"

"I'm saying we'll never keep up with Tom. It's best to admit that from the start—so we don't kill ourselves."

"But I thought the whole reason we were doing this was to spend time together, just the three of us?"

"Yeah, sure. All I'm saying is, unless Tom slows down some, it's gonna be just the two of us."

I shook my head in disbelief and dread. The only reason I agreed to this torture was to spend some quality time with Tom. Now Edmund was telling me that unless I was in decathlon shape, it probably wasn't going to happen. Maybe I could be picked off by a drive-by shooter to make the day complete.

By the time we arrived at Pioneer Park, the driving rain was driving harder. Tom was already performing the runner's ritual prerun warm-up muscle stretches. As I expected, Tom was wardrobed from head to toe in Dodgers issue cap, jacket, and pants.

"Hey guys! Wet enough for you?" Tom smirked as he placed his right leg far above his head, a posture I could only hope to achieve once I get to heaven and get a glorified body. (I believe the earthly model for the heavenly body is Gumby.)

Edmund joined in on the stretches, looking like he knew what he was doing—one more hint that I was to be the Village Idiot of this three-some.

"What's your plan for our run?" Edmund asked Tom, trying hard to downplay his enthusiasm and go for a more matter-of-fact,-I-jog-all-the-time-with-a-former-pro-athlete tone of voice.

"I thought we'd run up toward Nevada City for a few miles, and then circle back around toward Pine Woods. Actually, if you guys are up to it, we could run a route that would have us finish down at Starbucks in Pine Woods. It would probably add another mile to our run. What do you think?"

"I say, let's go for it!" Edmund replied, never giving a minute's thought to what this would be doing to my ability to participate.

Suddenly, I decided it was important for me to come clean. "I probably need to tell you guys something."

"What's on your mind, Bill?" Tom asked.

"I just want you guys to know that I haven't really jogged as much as usual lately, and I feel pretty out of shape."

"That's all right," Tom comforted.

"I guess I'm saying I might start lagging behind a little, so don't worry about me."

"We'll stay with you, brother, don't worry." Tom always seemed to know the right thing to say, one more reason I admired him so much.

I remember thinking right before we started running that I really wanted to ask Tom about how he had pulled his life so together. I thought it would make such a perfect topic of conversation as we jogged in the rain, side by side.

Of course, once we started running, I realized that *nothing* besides running could be attempted. Conversation? It took every ounce of oxygen I possessed to stay alive. Edmund really surprised me. I knew Tom was a big-time runner, but Edmund's ability to keep up with him was startling. When I first began, I carefully tried to sidestep every puddle of mud and water. But only seconds into the jog, as fatigue hit me full force, I recklessly abandoned my impulse to stay tidy. I went for survival. I hit puddles with the total of my tonnage, water splattering everywhere and mud slowly climbing up from my shoes to the lower portions of my sweatpants.

"You okay, Bill?" Tom asked about a minute into our run, as he slowed down to run alongside of me.

"Sure...no...probleh...Tohh..." I struggled to answer, while attempting to find air from some new source. It was clear I had only enough strength for one more sentence, so I knew this was my only chance with Tom.

"I...wanted...to...ask....you...about...how...you...seem...so...to geth...Wha...I...you...secre?"

That word "secret" would be the last one I would utter for the next several hours.

"Bill, that's a real good question, and I'm glad you asked it. Actually, I was wanting to talk to you about the exact same issue. I've noticed some of the ways you've been approaching life since the retreat and I think I can be of some—"

I was told later that this is what Tom said to me. My hearing ceased right after I had asked him my question. It wasn't only my hearing that left me. It was also my sight, my strength, and my heart.

When I was exactly over the largest rain puddle we had encountered, my body gave out and I plummeted face forward into the mud. As I fell, I pondered, *Perhaps God's love and grace will allow me to die by drowning in this dirty water, rather than face the excruciating pain of getting back up.*

The rest of the story was related to me later. My best friend, Edmund, apparently unaware of my collapse, kept running. But Tom stopped immediately. He quickly turned me over, rolling me out of the puddle at the same time. Since I had hit the mud square in the face, I looked a little like Al Jolson in *The Jazz Singer*, but I didn't even have the breath to ask for Mammy. I was out cold, bulky and cumbersome like a five-hundred-pound sack of flour, lying limp in the rainy beauty of Pioneer Park.

Tom yelled for Edmund to stop running. When Edmund realized what had happened, his face went ashen. "WHAT'S WRONG WITH BILL?" he screamed at the top of his lungs.

"Relax, Edmund, he's okay," Tom reassured.

"He looks dead," Edmund said solemnly, head bowed, hands folded in a prayerlike manner.

"He's not dead, he's just passed out," Tom replied. "But this is nothing to take lightly, so I want you to run back to the entrance, grab the pay phone, and call 911. I'll stay here with Bill and see if I can revive him, okay?"

"Gotcha." Edmund saluted in a military fashion as he ran off in the direction we had come from. Fortunately for me, I had collapsed one minute away from where we began.

As the story is told, the paramedics came to Pioneer Park in an effort to revive the White Whale that had been found beached in the foothills of the Sierra. They seemed concerned about some of my vital signs. For example, they couldn't find several.

And that is how I ended up in the hospital emergency room.
(The thing that *really* ticks me off is that I never got my latte.)

14

I came around completely before I got to the hospital, but I was so exhausted from my one-minute run that I closed my eyes and took a little nap. This wasn't easy, as the guys in the dark-blue jumpsuits kept trying to revive me—poking me, jabbing me, and asking me questions to keep me from my slumber.

I heard them muttering about pulse and "BP" and heart rate and temperature. Suddenly, me being a normal guy and all, the financial impact of this fiasco hit with the force of a Sherman tank.

I lifted my head. "Did Elizabeth Dole send you guys?" I asked.

"What?" replied one of the medics, a muscular sort in his mid-thirties.

"Are you from the Red Cross?" I tried another tact, still hoping for the best.

"No, we're not."

"Then all this stuff you guys are doing to me is going to be billed to my Blue Cross, right?"

"Most likely, if your Blue Cross plan covers these sorts of expenses. A lot of them don't."

"Thanks for the encouragement," I replied. "I'll take the modified plan, if that's all right with you guys. Don't pay me the slightest attention unless my heart stops, okay? *Nada*—unless I'm a flatliner."

"Well, actually, sir....Sir? Sir?" It was too late for conversation, as I was fast asleep. Sleep had always been such a good escape for me, and I knew it wouldn't let me down now.

I didn't stir again until I was transferred from the ambulance to the emergency room entrance at Pine Woods Memorial Hospital. I vaguely remember Tom and Edmund running alongside the gurney, responding to the nurse's questions. "Is he on any sort of medication, legal or illegal?"

I tried to picture Edmund, Tom, and I smoking mushrooms. It was funny and groovy, but it would never happen, not even back in the sixties. Apparently I giggled.

"He's coming back around, Doctor," I heard another nurse bark. I opened my eyes just in time to discover that they had removed my sweatshirt and T-shirt, and they were standing over me with those two electronic things they were planning to use to zap my chest! I bolted up on the gurney, suddenly wide awake. I sure didn't want to go home looking like a cinnamon crispa.

Once my eyes focused a little better and I discovered that what I thought were chest-zappers were really clipboards the attending nurses use to hold the forms which record the thousands of lines of data that they write down in preparation for submitting their itemized bill.

"Well, look who's here!" came a somewhat familiar voice from the foot of the bed. I looked down to see Dr. Graydon, also holding a clipboard, smiling broadly at me.

"All I can say is that it's a good thing it was raining this morning, Butterworth."

I didn't quite get the meaning of his statement. "Did the rain somehow save my life, Doc?"

"No, it had nothing to do with it, actually. What I was referring to was the fact that a sunny Saturday at ten-thirty in the morning would have found me on about the seventh fairway and there would have been no way I would have left my golf game to come attend to you. Your only chance would have been if I was playing poorly, and let me assure you, that rarely happens. After all, I am a doctor."

"Are you pulling my leg?" I asked.

"No, but I will," he kidded as he reached down, grabbed my right leg and gave it a yank.

"Dr. Graydon!" a nurse immediately protested. The jerking of my body threatened to disconnect me from my IV tubes.

"Oops," Dr. Graydon said in a halfhearted effort to apologize to the nurses. *Never mind me,* I thought. *I could be dying of IV deprivation, but apparently the important thing is to keep up the camaraderie with the staff.*

"And hey, what kind of a doctor says, 'Oops'?"

But the nurses smiled at Dr. Graydon's joke and stuck me with another IV needle. I wondered if they were smiling at the Doc or at the prospect of piercing me one more time. I've watched investigative reports on television concerning sadistic medical people.

I finally asked, "Am I okay, Doc?"

"Yes," Dr. Graydon replied. I breathed a huge sigh of relief.

"I think you just overexerted yourself out there, Bill. I've been speaking to your friends Edmund and Tom here, and they seem to agree that it's been quite some time since you've been running. So let me ask you, since no one else is quite certain about this, when *was* the last time you went jogging?"

"1981."

As if on cue, everyone hovering over my bed rolled his or her eyes in unison.

"Can I go home?" I asked.

"Actually, Bill, I'd like to keep you here overnight just to observe your progress. I'm not expecting anything to be wrong, but it's better to be safe, if you know what I mean."

I nodded the nod of a defeated man. Overnight in a hospital equals the cost of Christmas, the family vacation, new tires for the Honda, and that Troy Aikman replica jersey that I wanted to buy if I could somehow justify it in the budget.

"Will someone let my kids know I'm here without upsetting them too much?"

"I already spoke with them and they're just fine," came a voice. A blur of pastel green approached from my left.

"Edmund!" It was so good to see his reassuring smile as he switched places with one of the nurses, reached out, and squeezed my hand.

"Tom's wife is stopping by your house to pick your boys up, so they'll be here soon. I spoke to all of them and they're concerned, but they're fine."

"Tom's wife?"

"Yeah, I'm here, too, buddy," Tom spoke from the right side of the bed. "You gave us all a scare, Butterworth!" Tom had a way of joking in a good-natured way that still got his point across.

"Sorry, guys. I really didn't plan to do this. I guess I should've warmed up a little more."

"Yeah, like maybe fifteen years," offered one of the nurses as she left the room. I know she was thinking, *One more middle-aged guy who thinks he's under thirty.*

"Well, everything checks out okay," Dr. Graydon interrupted. "So I'd like to suggest that since we charge by the minute for the emergency room, how about if we move you upstairs to a regular room, where we only charge by the hour?"

Dr. Graydon's attempt at humor fell flat, if you ask me. The nurses, however, thought he was Steve Martin and howled like hyenas.

A nurse wheeled me to a semiprivate hospital room on the third floor. She sponge-washed all the mud off me, and then ordered me into one of those ridiculous hospital gowns that cover your front while providing hours of entertainment for anyone who happens to be behind you.

Once I was propped up in my bed, I looked out the window. It was still an overcast, gloomy day. *The perfect day to flirt with death,* I thought.

I winced, wondering how I could have done something so incredibly stupid so as to end up in the hospital, everyone worried, and me wearing one of Graydon's fully-ventilated aprons.

Glancing out the door of my room, I observed that no one wearing a hospital gown was moving past the door under their own power. They were either using walkers, or being wheeled along in wheelchairs, or worse yet, being rolled down the hall on gurneys, apparently heading for the dissecting room.

Hospitals have always given me the creeps. Becoming a full-fledged hospitalized human being suddenly felt overwhelming to me. There I sat, propped up in my sterile hospital bed, a tear threatening to roll down my cheek. I was a frightened, frazzled, and extremely frustrated man who would never pull the loose ends of life together, and who would surely be the laughingstock at his own reunion.

"Are you all right?"

It was Tom Graham's voice.

"Tom? I didn't realize you were here," I muttered, as I quickly dried my face with a sleeve of my hospital gown.

"We wouldn't leave you, buddy. Edmund is out at the pay phone making a few calls to our friends, letting them know what's going on and asking them to pray. I'm waiting here for Meg to bring your boys and then we'll leave you alone, if you prefer."

"No, no, that's all right, you can stay."

I turned my head and met the eyes of this guy I admired so much. As I did that, the waterworks returned, and I was utterly helpless to turn them off.

"Tom, my life is a mess," I sobbed. "Ever since the retreat I have tried *so hard* to get my life together, but it just hasn't happened. To be honest, it's only gotten worse. I mean, look at me." I pointed to my condition as a hospitalized stupid person.

"Bill, I want you to know that I've been watching you very closely since the retreat, and I agree with what you're saying. You have been trying your very best to get your life together." Tom's voice was warm, comforting, and reassuring.

"So why is it that my life is worse now than before?"

"Well, I can think of a couple of reasons why things are going the way they are," Tom offered. "Are you up to discussing this, or should we wait until later?"

"Now," I answered without a moment's hesitation. "Please tell me, Tom. I really need all the help I can get right now." I couldn't believe how desperate I sounded.

"Okay. First of all, you know that when you make some sort of spiritual commitment that the devil doesn't want you to succeed in all this stuff, right?"

I nodded.

"So he is gonna put all kinds of extra hassle in your way to keep you from accomplishing your goal."

"I sure have had my share of hassles," I admitted.

"I know. You should consider it a compliment that Satan is so interested in making sure that you fail. The Lord must have big things ahead for you."

I liked what I was hearing. Leave it to Tom to make the mess of my life into something positive. No wonder this guy was my hero.

"There's something else to consider, Bill. Only you know the answer to this question, but it appears to me that you've been trying to get it together completely on your own. Have you been attempting to trust God and rely on his power to get you on top of all this craziness?"

It didn't take me long to respond. I had been totally negligent of relying on the Lord. I was a one-man band, destined to fall through the floor of life's stage.

"That's a good point, Tom. I guess I have sorta neglected God's power in all this. Actually, I guess I was maybe…hoping to impress him."

"Well, remember, buddy, when it comes to supernatural power, we can only *receive* it, we cannot generate it."

I felt like C. S. Lewis was at my bedside, walking me through my grief observed.

On one hand, Tom's words were encouraging. But on the other hand, it wasn't the first time I came to this realization, so I had a bit of skepticism as to whether I would ever get this principle applied to my life.

In my defense, I have to say that I know lots of guys who have a similar struggle. We're just wired that way. We can solve any problem all by ourselves, thank you. We don't need a woman's help, we don't need the help of another man, and most unfortunately, we don't need any help from God.

Maybe that's why some of us guys make getting our lives together our life work instead of accepting that it's God's work within us.

My contemplation was interrupted by the sound of a crowd in the hallway. My boys rushed into the hospital room with genuine concern written all over their faces. They came in the door, interestingly enough, in order of ages:

BJ led the manly group, looking more upset than I'd ever seen him.

Brandon was next. It appeared to me that he was very pale.

Ben marched in, trying, but failing, to look brave.

Bo brought up the rear, and my little guy was in tears.

"Guys, I'm okay, I'm okay," I tried to console everyone at once. "I just pushed it a little bit, that's all. I can go home tomorrow, so there's no reason to be upset."

No reaction.

"Look—I'll quit the marathon stuff and stick to sprints."

That seemed to help a little. Bo cracked a smile. But still we all stared at one another in awkward silence.

"Can any of you tell me what's bothering you?"

The other three immediately turned to BJ, and he saw unquestionably that he was shouldering the responsibility as family spokesman. He took a couple of deep breaths and looked me square in the eyes: "Dad, we were afraid we were gonna lose you."

The younger ones started sobbing quietly at the mention of their unspoken fears.

"We don't know what we'd do without you," he continued. "I guess what we're saying is that we love you, and I guess we don't tell you like we should, but believe me, you got our attention with this one."

I looked straight down the line and saw the four sweetest faces I had ever seen.

"We just want to tell you that we know how hard you work to take care of us and we also know that you've been trying extra hard since that weekend you went away with all the other guys. We probably haven't been doing all that much to carry our weight around the house, and so, we want you to know that when you get back on your feet, we'll be a little more helpful."

After another period of silence, I asked softly, "When did you guys discuss all this stuff?"

"In the car with Mrs. Graham is when we started," BJ answered, as he turned to look at Meg Graham who stood outside the doorway.

"And once we got here, we had a talk with Edmund, too," BJ added.

I once again turned my attention to the doorway, and sure enough, Edmund stepped into view and smiled a best friend's smile.

The kids stood there silent, waiting.

"Come here, you four, come and give your old man a hug!"

My boys have never responded quicker.

I made myself a mental promise to *never forget* this moment.

—When BJ puts another dent in his clunker of a car, remember this moment.

—When Brandon plays his music at the decibel level of the Concorde, remember this moment.

—When Ben forgets to study for his midterm until ten minutes before the test, remember this moment.

—When Bo rigs my clock radio to wake me up with "Vaya Con Dios," remember this moment.

I admit, I still have a lot of life that needs to be gotten together.

But I've got a lot that I wouldn't trade for anything—not even for Tom's Dodger gear or Edmund's Lexus. Not even for an impressive new suit and a buff body to put in it in time for my reunion.

Besides, there *are* a few things that have actually come together lately as a result of my efforts:

—I'm excited about continuing my Wenesday morning group. Plus, I think I've solved the problem of getting up so early— I won't go to bed at all on Tuesday night!

—I'm doing a little better in my devotional life. Granted, I'm studying the *Comic Book Bible,* but it's a start.

—Instead of a couple of donuts in the morning, I've been having one donut and one bran muffin. It moves me.

—I've discovered what a great friend I have in Edmund. I may even hire him again next April when my taxes are due.

—Slowly but surely, I *am* learning to trust God for help.

I spent most of that day in the hospital reflecting on what a fortunate fellow I am. My kids love me just the way I am! In fact, why not just skip my reunion, and use the money I would save to take the kids to Disneyland? I'll probably have more fun with the Country Bears than I would have had with my classmates, anyway.

With God's help, I'll never stop trying to get my life together. But what I *really* need to prove this summer is that I can ride on Space Mountain without getting motion-sick or screaming so hard I lose my voice. And if my kids and I survive the rides, and if we time everything carefully, we can probably catch a Dodger game as well.

Granted, there's a chance that Sherry Rich and Ruth Jensen may be a bit disappointed. But that's a fantasy I'll just have to risk.

Because the best reunion I'll ever have is right here.

A Note from the Author:

A literary work of this magnitude will undoubtedly raise the inevitable question: *How much of this book is truth and how much of this book is fiction?* Perhaps some clarification is in order.

The town of Pine Woods is fictitious, but it is based on the town in which I currently reside. I changed the name to avoid the possibility of lawsuits, as well as eviction.

I really do have children, one daughter and four sons. However, in reality their names are Joy, Jesse, Jeffrey, John, and Joseph. Changing their names afforded me greater latitude in telling tales without the necessity of paying them off at even higher rates than I already do. They are wonderful kids, but they constantly threaten to call a press conference to clarify what is true versus what I make up in my vivid imagination.

Tom and Meg Graham and Edmund and Jenny Holmes are characters I created based on several friends I've had in the past or have now. These composite characters represent the best in friends, mentors, brothers, and sisters. Many of them will appear in future Butterworth Comedy Novels. I never dreamed I'd have my very own series (or that it would come in book form instead of the funny pages).

Yes, there really is a Bill Butterworth. He is me. I don't really teach public speaking at a college (although I did teach speech for eight years quite some time ago). Nowadays I make my living writing books like this one and traveling around the country making speeches (write to me if you'd like me to give a presentation to your group. But beware—I've been known to use humor in my talks).

The main character in this book is exaggerated in many ways. I'd like to think I have it a little more together than the Bill in the story, but frankly I have days that make the fictional Butterworth's life look like heaven.

So, in truth, I am actually learning the lesson of this novel. The apostle Paul tells us to "Be strong in the Lord, and in the strength of His might" (Ephesians 6:10 NASB). I daily fight the human urge to live life under my own power. When I live in His strength, I make great strides toward getting my life together.

Finally, there really are teams called the Dodgers and the Cowboys. They are from Los Angeles and Dallas, respectively. And, as anyone like me who actually grew up in Philadelphia knows, there really are Tasty-kakes.